THE CHERRY VALLEY MIDDLE SCHOOL NEWS

DEAR KNOW-IT-ALL!

★ ★ ★

SET THE RECORD STRAIGHT!

by RACHEL WISE

Simon Spotlight

New York London Toronto Sydney New Delhi

SIMON SPOTLIGHT

An imprint of Simon & Schuster
Children's Publishing Division
1230 Avenue of the Americas,
New York, New York 10020
Copyright © 2012 by Simon & Schuster,
Inc. All rights reserved, including the
right of reproduction in whole or in
part in any form.
SIMON SPOTLIGHT and colophon are
registered trademarks of
Simon & Schuster, Inc.
Text by Elizabeth Doyle Carey
Designed by Laura L. DiSiena

For information about special discounts
for bulk purchases, please contact
Simon & Schuster Special Sales at
1-866-506-1949 or
business@simonandschuster.com.
Manufactured in the United States of
America 0612 FFG
First Edition 10 9 8 7 6 5 4 3 2 1
ISBN 978-1-4424-4445-4 (pbk)
ISBN 978-1-4424-5383-8 (hc)
ISBN 978-1-4424-4446-1 (eBook)
Library of Congress Control Number
2011943080

Chapter 1

KIDS TIRED OF TERRIBLE FOOD, BEG FOR MERCY

Can you keep a secret? I can't! I'm a journalist, and journalists are all about making secrets public.

Anyway, it kills me that I have to keep a major secret from almost everyone I know. Even my best friend, Hailey Jones. But I will tell *you*, if you promise not to tell anyone, okay?

Here it is: I am Dear Know-It-All.

Dear Know-It-All is the advice column in our school newspaper, the *Cherry Valley Voice*. Kids write in with questions about everything from homework to love lives to troubles at home. And each year one of the kids on the newspaper staff is chosen to anonymously write the answers, and this year it's me! Can you believe it? I myself was shocked when Mr. Trigg, our faculty advisor, called me at home to ask me to do it. But it's pretty fun, and an honor, even if it's a lot of responsibility.

In my first column, I answered a letter from someone asking what they should do if they liked their best friend's crush. Then I discovered by accident that it was Hailey writing in about liking *my* crush, Michael Lawrence! So after lots of angst, and a lot of thinking on my part, I wrote a column telling her to go for it— all's fair in love and war and all that—and then I held my breath to see what would happen. Hailey ended up confessing to me that she'd written the letter to Dear Know-It-All, and I had to pretend I didn't already know. The good thing was, in the end, she decided she didn't really like Michael, anyway. Phew! 'Cause I still do! But that's kind of another secret, okay?

So, as you can see, it's crazy stuff. If I wrote it up as a story for the *Cherry Valley Voice*, the headline would be ***Advice Columnist Caught in Love Triangle***. I love writing headlines, by the way. It's one of my greatest strengths as a journalist.

Our new issue comes out today, and I can't wait to see what people think of my latest column! Part of my job as Dear Know-It-All is to make my columns "jazzy." This one is jazzy all right! I really went all out and gave some pretty rad advice, if I do say so myself. I think it will have everyone talking. Here's what it was: A girl (who called herself Tired of Waiting) had written in to say she had had a crush on a guy for a long time and was tired of waiting for him to notice or to ask her out. She wasn't sure he even knew she walked on the planet, let alone liked him.

I had (anonymously, of course) replied that in this day and age, it wasn't all up to the guy. She should be a modern girl and just take charge and ask him out herself. I was pretty proud of that answer. It was sassy and modern and brave, not to mention well-written, if I do say so myself. The funny thing is, I've been in the same situation for years and I would never dare to ask Michael out, but that's because I'm such a chicken. I've learned that I can *give* pretty good advice. Following it is a whole other story!

Anyway, we always have a newspaper staff meeting in the afternoon, either on the day of or the day after the new issue of the *Cherry Valley Voice* comes out. Mr. Trigg likes everyone to have a chance to read it and get a sense of what our readership thinks of it. Then we all get together with him and our editor in chief (the job I want next year, if Michael doesn't get it!), and share info and brainstorm about our next issue, which we have to start on right away.

A couple of issues ago Michael and I coreported and cowrote a really big article on our school's new curriculum, and the article was a huge success. Mr. Trigg decided Michael and I are a great team—love that!—and he asked us to come up with another "blockbuster example of investigative journalism" for the meeting today. Mr. Trigg has a pretty funny way of talking sometimes. But it's pretty cool he chose us for another feature story. The only thing was, we were stumped for a topic.

Michael and I had made a plan to meet for lunch in the cafeteria to brainstorm. We started hanging out more after we wrote our last article together, but it's still pretty major for me to be going to lunch with Michael Lawrence, love of my life. The weird thing is, though, it's kind of like there are two Michael Lawrences. There's Michael my crush, whom I've loved since I was six (even though he caught me eating paste in kindergarten—I swear, I thought it was frosting—and has called me Pasty ever since) and who is just the cutest, coolest guy on the planet who makes my stomach go *swoosh*. Then there's Michael my writing partner, with whom I fight and negotiate with for assignments and about fact-checking, and stress over sources and all kinds of unromantic stuff. Then he's just kind of a friend. It's hard to believe that those two Michaels are the same guy.

Anyway, lunch. We got on the cafeteria line and were brainstorming the whole way, stopping occasionally to eavesdrop on people who were talking about the new issue of the *Voice*.

"What about something on allergy medication and how suddenly everyone has allergies? We could interview the school nurse and my pediatrician." Michael's dark eyebrows were bunched in thought, and his bright blue eyes narrowed as he considered the story's angles.

"Hm. That could be good," I said, distracted as I searched hopelessly for something to put on my tray. Now, I am a big eater. I'm tall, but I'm pretty thin. I am not picky, and I love food and need to eat often to keep my stomach full, otherwise it grumbles noisily and embarrasses me. But lately I've just been stumped by or grossed out with the cafeteria. Like today, here were the choices: a limp iceberg lettuce salad, orange JELL-O, crunchy Rice Krispies Treats, dry-looking mac and cheese, and tofu dogs—yuck! ***Kitchen Staff Poisons School Kids with Barfy Lunch!***

I looked to see what Michael was getting and saw that he was taking one of everything.

"Hungry?" I asked.

"Why? You want me to share this food with you too, Snacky?" His eyes twinkled as he teased me. Michael comes up with new nicknames for me all the time. It used to really bother me, but Hailey said that he does it because he likes me. If that's true then I don't mind being called things like Snacky. Well, not too much.

Michael has had to share his snacks with me on a few occasions when I got hungry and my stomach growled. I still get embarrassed by it.

"No, I am perfectly capable of supplying myself with the appropriate amount of nutrition that my growing body needs, thank you. I'm just not finding anything that appeals to me, and I'm surprised that you're finding so much."

"Well, the thing to do is take one of everything, then take two bites until it grosses you out, and move on to the next thing. You can get pretty full doing that." He grinned.

"Okaaay," I said. I wasn't convinced I should take gross food at all, but if it worked for Michael . . .

After loading up my tray with one of everything, I looked around for a good place to sit while Michael got milk. It would have to be close by, because the tray was very heavy. Across the room I spied Hailey waving at me to join her. By the way, I still feel a little nervous when Hailey and Michael are together—like I have to watch my back. I do believe Hailey when she swears she's over him, but then that also annoys me, because who could ever get over Michael Lawrence? But Hailey is my best friend, so I have to trust her.

Anyway, I called over to Michael, "Let's sit with Hailey," and he nodded.

I crossed the room, my full tray held high over people's heads, and about halfway there I overheard some kids talking about the new Dear Know-It-All column. Of course I slowed down.

"I would never ask a boy out!" said one of the girls, Tracey, from my math class.

She and her friends had a copy of the *Voice* laid out on their table in front of them and they were all looking at it.

"I would!" said a girl I didn't know.

I slowed down to a crawl, acting like I was looking for a spot to sit.

"Only if you had gone out with him already first, when *he'd* asked," said Kim, a pretty girl from my language arts class.

Hmm. She had a pretty good point. Anyway, at least my answer had gotten people talking.

I walked toward Hailey. At another table there were a bunch of boys talking about the column. I paused again. I love hearing people talk about the column, because no one knows it's me who wrote it. Plus, I'm curious to know what people think.

"Dude, no way! Uh-uh." Jack Francis, from my homeroom, was shaking his head. "I would never say yes to a girl if she'd ask me out."

He is such a nerd. I wanted to say, *Don't worry, buddy. It's not gonna happen, anyway*, but I restrained myself.

One of his friends was looking kind of thoughtful. "I would say yes. I mean, why does it always have to be us doing the asking?" he asked.

Bingo, brother! My point exactly. I smiled at him in gratitude, but then caught myself. I was supposed to be anonymous!

"I just think that it's a totally weird move if a girl does that," Jack said. "It's just not the way it's done."

Uh-oh. I took a deep breath and kept walking, reminding myself that part of being a journalist is provoking conversation. And anyway, why is that "the way it's done"? Says who, I'd like to know.

". . . really bad advice!" I heard someone say

as I passed another table. My stomach clenched. Were they talking about the Dear Know-It-All column too? Ugh. Maybe I'd been too daring. But everyone sure was talking about it!

I reached Hailey and dropped my tray onto the table with relief, and mostly because it was so heavy from taking one of everything. As I did so, everything jostled and mixed all together in a revolting fashion: apple juice spilled over iceberg, JELL-O in the mac and cheese—just gross.

"Argh!" I cried. This was turning into a very bad lunch in all ways.

"Finally!" said Hailey.

"Why 'finally'?" I asked, pulling out my chair and sitting down heavily.

"I have major news."

"Okay, ladies, *bon appétit!*" said Michael, placing his tray next to mine on the table and sitting down.

"What?" I asked Hailey.

She shook her head in annoyance. "Can't say now," she whispered, flicking her eyes toward Michael.

Double ugh! I'd never been annoyed to see Michael before, but now I was.

I glanced down at my tray. It looked disgusting. I didn't know where to begin.

"I meant two bites of each thing at a time, not mixed all together, Pasty," Michael said, shaking his head and laughing.

"Ha-ha," I said. I took a deep breath and pulled my long, brown hair into a ponytail while deciding what to tackle first.

Suddenly I felt a nudge. I looked down, and Michael had a granola bar in his hand and he was poking me with it. I wanted to say no, just on principle, but I knew I'd be starving before too long, so I reached out and took it.

"Thanks," I muttered, feeling grumpy.

"I carry them for you," said Michael, grinning.

"Yeah, right," I said, annoyed that he was teasing me about my appetite again.

"For real," Michael insisted, serious now.

Oh. Was this a good thing or a bad thing? I'd need to dissect it with Hailey later and decide. Either Michael worried that I was a liability when hungry and needed to be appeased, or he was being considerate. Or maybe both. Either way it was probably good that he was thinking about me. Right? Or maybe what he was thinking was that I was a starving pig! Oh brother. Either way, I was hungry. ***Starving Journalist Goes on Eating Spree! Nothing Is Safe!***

I unwrapped the granola bar and glanced at Hailey's tray. "What did you have?" I asked her, biting into the bar.

"Rice," she said, shrugging.

"Just rice?"

Hailey nodded. "With some butter and salt on it."

I chewed thoughtfully. "This is not a third-world country, you know. We have more than just rice to eat." That's something Hailey's mom always said to her.

"The food is such a bummer. There's never anything I want. I'm actually thrilled when they have rice," said Hailey. "I keep telling you to do an article on that! How bad the food is!"

I turned to her midbite, with half the granola bar hanging out of my mouth, and then looked at

Michael with wide eyes. "Bingo!" I said through the rolled oats. ***Kids Tired of Terrible Food, Beg for Mercy.***

Michael nodded and then finished chewing before speaking. He wiped his mouth with his napkin and then pushed his tray away. (Did I mention he has great manners?)

"Great idea, Hails," he said. "'Tuna Surprise Is a Real Surprise!' 'Booger Burgers Make us Barf!'"

Hails? That's *my* nickname for her. Grrr. Now all of me was growling, not just my stomach.

Hailey smiled and fluffed her short blonde hair with her fingers. I squinted at her to see if she was flirting, but she looked innocent. How could she really not like Michael? He was so perfect. . . .

"I said it a couple of weeks ago. I would have thought you'd remembered," she said to him.

Phew. I was glad Michael hadn't. That meant he didn't pay *too* much attention to what she said. And he was too busy remembering granola bars for me.

"It's a good idea," I said. "We'll present it at the meeting today and see what Trigger thinks." I reached into my messenger bag for my trusty note-book. I made a note on my to-do list, snapped the book shut, and placed it in the bag. Nothing gets remembered unless I write it down, even though Michael teases me for it. He thinks I'm just a bad listener, but I don't care. This is just how my brain works.

I finished my granola bar and then put the empty wrapper onto my tray. True to his word, Michael had sampled everything on his tray exactly twice.

"I've gotta run," he said. "I'm meeting Jeff to go over the names in the team photos for the year-book."

Jeff Perry is in our grade, and he's one of Michael's best friends. He's the photographer for the *Cherry Valley Voice* and always has a big cam-era slung over his narrow shoulder or around his skinny neck. He's pretty funny, but sometimes you wish he didn't take quite so many photos. They don't always turn out so great, and he isn't shy about posting them on Buddybook. My dream is that one day Hailey will decide she loves him. I think they'd be great together. And then I really wouldn't have to worry about Michael.

"See you at the meeting," I said to Michael.

When Michael had left, Hailey turned to me. "I thought he'd never leave," she said.

Chapter 2

SPIES CAUGHT MIDTRANSFER, COVERS BLOWN!

★ ★ ★

"What is *up*?" I asked Hailey. "The suspense is killing me!"

Hailey's eyes shone brightly as she smiled at me. "I'm in love! And I'm going to ask him out! Just like they said in Dear Know-It-All!"

Huh?

My shock quickly turned to action. "Whoa, tiger! Slow down! *You* wrote that letter to Dear Know-It-All? You're Tired of Waiting?!"

Hailey waved her hand impatiently. "No, I didn't write it, but, I mean, the advice applies, right? Do you know Scott Parker? On the boys' varsity soccer team?"

Did I mention that Hailey is a soccer nut?

She's cocaptain of the girls' varsity team, and she's only in seventh grade. She's in sick shape, totally muscle, even though she's very petite.

I nodded. I did know who Scott Parker was. Actually, we'd been at nursery school together, but I didn't know him well, though.

"Yeah, he's really cute!" I said. I remembered him as being very quiet and shy, not like Hailey at all, but maybe he'd outgrown it.

Hailey nodded, grinning again. "Waaay cute!" She sighed and crossed her arms. "And I'm going to ask him out!"

Oh. This did not seem like a good idea. From what I knew, Scott was not the kind of guy who girls asked out; I thought he was way too shy. Plus, did he even know Hailey or had she even talked to him? I had to stop her. "Wait. Hailey. Why rush into this? You've only just decided that you like him, right? Slow down and take your time. Let him get to know you a little bit." I gulped. I'd felt so breezy and confident writing that column, but now that it was in practice, I could see that maybe not *all* boys are the type who girls should ask out.

Anyway, it wasn't like Hailey was pining away for him like Tired of Waiting was for her guy.

I looked at Hailey, and she was kind of pouting. "Why? Do you think he'd say no if I asked?"

Poor Hailey. She finally likes someone legit (as in, someone who has not been my crush for the past seven years), and now I'm telling her not to go for it. Or, at least, not yet.

I scrambled to make her feel better. "No. I just think . . . he's not the type of guy that . . ."

Hailey narrowed her eyes at me. "Do you think he's a jerk?" she asked.

"No! I barely know the guy!" I protested. Oh boy. I was really getting myself in trouble here. "Look, Hails, just take it slow. Baby steps. You've just decided you like him. Live with it for a week and then we'll make a plan, okay?"

"We?" said Hailey.

"Yes, we." I patted her on the arm, and smiled.

Hailey exhaled. "Okay. But I'm not as patient as you are."

"I know. Seven years is a long time to wait. But he's worth it!"

Hailey laughed, and we began to collect our trays. "Do you need some help?" she asked, eyeing my pile.

"Thanks. That would be great." I shifted the JELL-O and the little plate with a Rice Krispies treat on it onto Hailey's plate, then I turned to hoist my messenger bag from the floor. When I looked back at Hailey, she was eating the Rice Krispies Treat and had the JELL-O in her other hand.

"Hailey!" I cried.

She whipped her head around in surprise. "What?!"

"I thought you meant if I needed help carrying it, not eating it!"

Hailey blushed. "Sorry. I didn't see these when I was up there, though. And you know how I love—"

"High-fructose corn syrup. I know. But to eat all that stuff at once, that's just gross. Let's go."

Reluctantly, Hailey stood, still chewing, and we deposited our trays and then left the cafeteria without mishap.

We still had a little time before the next period, so as we walked to our next class, I tried to boost

Hailey's confidence but warned her to still be cautious. I felt like I'd been too hasty at lunch, and I didn't want to make her feel badly (*Advice Columnist Retracts Advice!*). "Listen, Hails, that letter . . . the Dear Know-It-All thing. That girl . . . It sounded like she had liked that guy for a really long time. She was lovelorn and devoted, she was 'tired of waiting.' But you've just *started* liking Scott. Like, hello—*new crush!* So I think you need to play it cool a little, you know? Get to know him, find out what you have in common besides soccer. Maybe first come up with a casual group plan with a bunch of friends, okay?" I turned to look at Hailey and found her walking very close to me, peering at me intently.

"What?" I said, pulling back in surprise.

Hailey wagged her finger at me. "Wait a second! I know who you are! Now it all makes sense!'

Oh my goodness. Panic coursed through my veins. What did I say that finally revealed I'm Dear Know-It-All? I gulped.

Hailey stopped dead in her tracks with an incredulous smile on her face. "You're *Tired of*

Waiting! Tired of Waiting for Michael Lawrence! I should have known!"

I laughed weakly. "Oh, yeah. Ha-ha." Relief washed over me as I realized my cover was safe, for now anyway. "Right. That was me—Not."

Hailey looked at me suspiciously. "Are you sure?"

"Yes. Positive. Trust me. I'd have asked my best friend for advice first, obviously!" I gave her a soft punch on the upper arm.

Hailey gave me another look. "You actually *give* really good advice, you know. Maybe next year they'll ask *you* to be the Dear Know-It-All!" And she slapped me on the back and then turned into the science lab. "Ha-ha! As if!" she called over her shoulder, laughing.

"Thanks!" I called after her. "Great idea!" Sheesh! That was a really close call. But why 'as if'? Sure, I didn't love being Dear Know-It-All, but did I stink at it? Why didn't she think I was qualified? Now I was annoyed again.

I walked to language arts thinking about Tired, the real Tired of Waiting. I wondered what had happened, if she had asked her guy out after all, and if so, how it had turned out. I felt kind of sick about my pithy advice ("pithy" is Mr. Trigg's favorite word, by the way). It means you say something strongly and forcefully, like you're sure of it. But, really, what did I know about asking out boys?

For about the one millionth time, I thought about what a terrible choice I was to write this column. After all, I can barely lead my own life, let alone tell other people how to lead theirs! And, anyway, my expertise is facts. That's why I like journalism. It's all about what really happened, not about feelings or things that are hard to prove. So even though it's fun and a huge honor to write Dear Know-It-All, I do secretly kind of hate having to do it.

After school I hustled to the *Cherry Valley Voice* office for our staff meeting. I was hoping to get there early and quickly touch base with Mr. Trigg about the Dear Know-It-All reaction. Since he's the only person besides my mom who knows that I write it, I love chatting with him about it (except for when I'm late on my deadlines; then I avoid him like the plague!). I was really nervous to hear what he'd heard or what he'd thought. My stomach had butterflies in it and I prayed no one was in the office to prevent us from talking.

I was lucky. I flew past the door and the newsroom was still empty. Mr. Trigg was at his desk in his little private office at the back of the room.

"Mr. T.!" I called.

"Ms. Martone!"

I crossed the room quickly and poked my head into his office, which is filled with World War II memorabilia. He is British and obsessed with journalism, World War II, and Winston Churchill—not necessarily in that order. A huge British government war poster hung over his desk. It said, "*Your* Courage, *Your* Cheerfulness, *Your* Resolution Will Bring Us Victory." I gulped.

"What did you think of the column?" I whispered.

It's not like he hasn't been involved with it every step of the way. Mr. Trigg has to download the anonymous Dear Know-It-All e-mails from the server (there's a scrambler to hide the senders' e-mail addresses), and he has to forward to me any letters submitted to the Know-It-All mailbox outside the *Cherry Valley Voice* office. He also has to approve my choice of letter for each column and read my answer before it's printed. But he actually lets me have a lot of leeway in what I write. The advice is all me.

He smiled. "Wonderful. And lots of chatter."

I nodded. "But not all of it positive."

"That happens. We just want to get people talking, debating, thinking, without being inappropriate or irresponsible. That's our job as journos, right?" He winked at me.

I tried to look more confident than I felt. If he wasn't worried, then why should I be worried? "Righty-ho, then!" I said, using one of his expressions back at him. Trigger guffawed his trademark horsey laugh.

"Wonderful, just wonderful," he said, taking out a hanky and blowing his nose. "Now, Ms. Martone, I will be announcing this in the meeting, but just to let you know, I am out of town for a few days this week, starting tomorrow. Heading to a newspaper conference in Washington, DC. I'll be back

Monday. I am reachable by e-mail. . . ." And with that he held up a note for me to read, winking and nodding while he kept talking. It said, "KNOW-IT-ALL PASSWORD ON SERVER: wwiinston."

"And you can leave me a note in my mailbox . . ." he continued, handing me a key with a London taxi keychain (clearly the key to the Know-It-All mailbox). Winking and nodding again, he then handed me a manila envelope containing this week's submission letters so far. Then he continued, talking about other general newspaper details.

Did I mention Mr. Trigg loves cloak-and-dagger stuff? I think he actually wishes he were a spy. Here he is in an empty newsroom, where he easily could say whatever he wanted without revealing who I am, or he could have left an envelope in my mailbox with both the key and the password. But instead he chooses to stage the whole thing like a spy exchange, as if the office is bugged by . . . the enemy? Which is who, exactly?

The door opened in the outer office behind me, and kids began to arrive for the meeting. I jammed the keychain and envelope down into my messenger bag. *Spies Caught Midtransfer, Covers Blown!*

"Okay, Mr. Trigg. Have a great trip! I'll be in touch if I need you!" I winked and nodded, and then backed out of the room while he sat at his desk, grinning and winking, obviously pleased that the whole "transfer" had gone so well. I had to give the guy credit for how he had managed to merge his two passions—WWII and Winston— into a password. Clever.

Out in the *Voice* office, I chose a seat on a little beat-up couch and put my messenger bag next to me to save a spot for Michael. I wondered vaguely if he'd realize I loved him just by the fact I'd saved him a seat. Nah. Probably not, I decided. He sure didn't act lovey-dovey when he rushed in at the last minute.

"Thanks, Paste," he said. I love having a nick-name for my nickname. Not.

The meeting went well. Everyone was pleased with the new issue and had heard good feedback out around school. Mr. Trigg had even had a call from Mr. Pfeiffer, the principal, to say how great he thought the new issue was. (Phew!) Most of the other writers and editors said that lots of people were talking about Dear Know-It-All. When they said this, they looked around the room searchingly (with an anonymous writer, everyone was suspicious of everyone else), but I kept my cool, even when Katherine Thomas mentioned she'd heard a lot of people saying it was bad advice. I gulped.

"Please keep me apprised of anything more you hear," said Mr. Trigg, moving on before everyone started to guess who wrote the column, which happened after almost every meeting.

Next it was time to brainstorm article topics for the next issue. I let Michael raise his hand to present our idea.

"We're thinking 'School Lunch and Why It's So Gross,'" said Michael.

A couple of kids clapped, and Jeff let out a long whistle of approval. Michael and I grinned.

Mr. Trigg folded his arms tightly and tapped his chin with his index finger. That's what he does when he's thinking. "Yesss . . ." he said slowly, drawing out the word. "But let's not say that's definitely the thesis and certainly not the headline. Start out with some reporting, and when I get back from my trip, we'll review what you've discovered, all righty? Next?" Mr. Trigg turned away.

Michael and I looked at each other, a little surprised Trigger hadn't embraced our idea as fully as we'd expected.

"Weird," I said.

Michael shrugged. "Do you think he likes the food?"

I giggled. "Probably. What with his history of war rations . . ." Mr. Trigg hadn't lived through World War II, so I was only joking.

Michael didn't laugh, though. He was distracted, thinking.

I sighed.

Men. Boys. They're so unpredictable.

Chapter 3

ADVICE COLUMNIST A SHAM, READERS REVOLT!

The next day was busy from start to finish. I raced from class to class, wolfed down a plate of rice with butter and salt (thanks for the recipe, Hailey), and at the very end of the day, commandoed past the *Cherry Valley Voice* office and swiped a letter from the Dear Know-It-All mailbox when no one was around.

That night, after I had finished my homework and read the days' blogs and news websites, which is always my reward for finishing my homework, I pulled out the manila envelope from Trigger and took out the letters inside. I had had piles of homework the night before and hadn't had a chance to look through the package

Trigger had given me. (Well, okay, I kind of did have time, but I procrastinated. I was still queasy about the feedback from my printed answer from this week's column, and I couldn't face a new set of letters.)

There weren't too many in his package—four, in fact—and I read through them quickly, having by now realized that most Dear Know-It-All letters fall into strict categories. They are: the medical ("What can I do about my acne?" or "How can I grow taller?"), the standard domestic drama ("I hate my little brother, he's always fooling around with my stuff"), the nerdy ("What are colleges really looking for in a candidate?"), and the lovelorn ("No boys like me").

The fifth letter was the one I had picked up from the mailbox today. It was handwritten and in an envelope, with a return address, and it turned out that it didn't fall into any of those categories.

It was from Tired of Waiting.

I turned the envelope over in my hands, and paused. I was dying for feedback, but what if it wasn't good? Or maybe it was great! Maybe she'd asked him out, and he'd said yes! I almost ripped it open, but my stomach clenched. Oh gosh. I couldn't do it!

I sat with the letter in my hand, staring off into space. What if . . . ? What if . . . ?

Finally, I shook my head. Your *Courage,* Your *Cheerfulness,* Your *Resolution Will Bring Us Victory,* I thought. I ripped open the letter, like I was tearing off an old BAND-AID, and my eyes skimmed it quickly. It said:

Dear Know NOTHING AT ALL,

Thanks a lot. I asked out my crush, and he not only said no, he told all his friends. And now they all laugh at me whenever I walk by. And he doesn't even talk to me.

Thanks for nothing.

Tired of Bad Advice

Oh no! I collapsed into a heap and threw down the letter, as if it had burned me. My hand flew to cover my mouth in shock, and I sat there, slumped in my chair while panic coursed through my veins. This was what I'd been dreading ever since I'd agreed to write the Dear Know-It-All column a month ago. I had given bad advice, and someone had taken it, and now I'd wrecked her life! *Advice Columnist a Sham, Readers Revolt!*

My first thought was, *Thank goodness I stopped Hailey before she went too far!* I could only imagine what Scott would have done if she'd asked him out, point-blank. But poor Tired!

There was a knock on my door, and it opened, without me even saying, "Come in." It was my sister, Allie, who is obsessed with her own privacy but doesn't care a bit about anyone else's.

"Hey, I know you're Ms. Blog, and I was wondering . . ." Suddenly Allie stopped and actually looked at me for a change. "What's wrong? You look like your best friend just died!"

"Oh, it's nothing. It's just . . . middle-school drama, you know." I tried to smooth over it. The last thing I need is Allie finding out that I'm Dear Know-It-All, and a mediocre one at that. She'd have a field day critiquing my work and torturing me.

She narrowed her eyes suspiciously. Allie has a better nose for news than I do, actually. She runs the high school's website, the student section, and so I guess she is kind of involved in current events. But what she mostly does is text about events and post stuff on Buddybook, and talk on the phone with her friends, all of whom she likes better than she likes me.

"Does this have anything to do with Crushie Crusherson?" Allie pressed.

She knows I like Michael. And she's friends with his older brothers, so she has access to him, which really scares me. I'm always praying she doesn't say anything to him if she sees him.

"No." I sighed impatiently.

"Hailey?"

"No, stop fishing! It's nothing."

Allie stared me down, and I looked away. I would not crack, even if she gave me a major interrogation.

Suddenly her phone began ringing, down the hall in her room. Out of the corner of my eye, I saw her react to it, then will herself to remain standing in my doorway, staring me down. Once, twice, three times . . .

And then *Allie* cracked!

"Oh, whatever!" And she stormed down the hall to her room. I was pleased with my steely nerve, and also grateful to whomever it was who had called her.

I looked back at the letter from Tired. I didn't know what to do. My first instinct was to call, e-mail, or write to her, but I had no idea how to get in touch with her. I couldn't publish an apology in the *Cherry Valley Voice* because we weren't due for another issue of the paper until the week after next. Plus, it wouldn't exactly make me look good to issue an apology in the third column I ever wrote.

I thought about calling Mr. Trigg, but that seemed babyish, like I was running to my mommy for help. Speaking of which, I thought of telling my mom. She is the one person besides Mr. Trigg who knows that I am Dear Know-It-All, but we never discuss it because she knows I need to remain mum on the subject. But maybe. . . or Hailey? Could I just fess up to it all? Gosh, I felt like I really needed her support right now. But . . .

No.

It wasn't that serious. I could handle it. I would just chalk this up to a learning experience. My future advice should just avoid concrete tips and instead focus on telling people to do what they feel is right. That way I'm not on the hook. I'll just kind of coast through this assignment. That's all.

I sighed heavily, knowing that was a cop-out, and I was not feeling better. I couldn't stop wondering who Tired was and who she liked. And what kind of mean boy would treat a girl like that?

"Hey." Allie was back in my doorway.

"Hey," I said.

"Listen, if you want me to, I can tell little Mikey's brothers that you like him. That way maybe he'll—"

"No!" I bellowed, jumping out of my seat and running toward Allie. "No way!"

Allie looked shocked. "Okay, okay. Sheesh! I was just trying to help. Sometimes if you do a little work behind the scenes . . ."

"No! Just . . . no." I closed my eyes.

"Fine, whatevs." Allie was not one to dwell on other people's problems. Well, unless they were her friends. She certainly wasn't going to dwell on mine. She abruptly switched gears. "Listen, I need to post a link on the high-school website to a blog or another site that has healthy snack recipes. I thought with all your Internet-ting around, you might have seen something." Allie folded her arms across her chest and leaned against the doorway.

My blood was still boiling, and I really wasn't in the mood to help her now.

"I don't know. I'll think about it," I said. I slid past her and headed downstairs for a snack.

"Think fast," she said, and she returned to her room.

Downstairs in the kitchen, I found a banana

and some peanut butter and raisins, and made my version of ants on a log.

"Sam, honey? Is that you?" my mother called from the den, which is also her office.

"Hi, Mom," I said. I tried not to sound sad, or she'd come in here to try to pry it out of me.

Which, of course, she did, anyway.

"What's wrong?" she asked, climbing the few stairs from the den to our kitchen.

"Nothing," I lied.

She put her lips to my forehead to see if I had a fever, but I squirmed away, so she sat down next to me at the kitchen table and then propped her chin onto her hands. My mom is a freelance accountant and bookkeeper, so she loves concrete facts as much as I do, even though hers are numbers and mine are words.

"Is everything okay with Hailey?" she asked.

"Yeah, and school's fine, and everything's fine," I said.

"How about the paper?" she asked. Then she dropped her voice to a whisper, "And the column?"

Typical. My mom has ESP, I'm sure of it.

How else could she hit the nail on the head within the first two minutes?

"It's . . . okay," I said.

Now my mom knew she was on to something. She leaned in closer, still whispering, "Are the letters tough?"

I nodded, and put my finger to my lips. I didn't want Allie to hear anything. Not that she could, all the way upstairs, but still.

"Hard to give advice?" she asked again.

I nodded again.

She sighed. "I know how you feel. It's kind of like being a parent," she said.

Hmm. Now this might be interesting. "How?" I asked in a normal voice. Allie wouldn't know what we were talking about, anyway. Besides, even if it crossed her mind that I was Dear Know-It-All, she'd probably laugh off the whole idea, thinking I wasn't qualified.

My mom continued. "People need to learn from their own mistakes. You can't protect them from everything. You need to let them find their own way. That's why I think it's important to keep advice open-ended, unless you have a very strong conviction about something. I mean, if an issue is black and white—like, don't cheat, don't steal, don't smoke—by all means give specific advice. But when it comes to choosing a path, sometimes people have to go through a process on their own."

"Okay," I said. "But then what do I tell people to do? It would be kind of a lame column if all I said was, 'Follow your heart.'"

"Would it?" my mom asked.

I shrugged. "Most of the time, yes."

My mom thought for a minute. "Then I guess . . . just be conservative. Don't tell anyone to do anything you wouldn't do yourself."

Oh great. Now she tells me. I sighed.

"Too late?" she asked with a smile.

I nodded.

"Oh boy. Can you fix it?" she asked.

"I don't know. Maybe."

"Well, it's never too late to try," she said. She walked over to give me a hug. I rested my head against her shoulder. She's still a little taller than I am. It was relaxing.

"Thanks," I said, pulling away.

"Thanks for letting me hug you," she said with a wink.

"Anytime," I said with a smile.

I climbed the stairs feeling a little better. From now on, I would keep my advice open-ended and not recommend that people do anything I wouldn't do. That was a good rule of thumb. And maybe there was a way I could get an apology note to Tired. I'd ask Mr. Trigg when he got back. It could certainly wait a few days. It's never too late to try!

Journalist Saves Sinking Ship.

Feeling charitable, I knocked and opened Allie's door.

"Hello? Privacy?" she said, without turning around from her computer screen.

I rolled my eyes. "Google someone named Mrs. Moseby. She has healthy snacks on her family cooking blog."

I started to close the door, and Allie said, "What were you and Mom whispering about down there?"

ARGH! See what I mean about a nose for news? "Nothing," I said.

"Yeah, right," replied Allie.

I closed the door and went to my room to get changed for bed. On my computer I saw that Hailey had IM'd me, so I clicked to read it.

Hellllppp! I think he likes someone else!!!!

Scott Parker, of course.

I couldn't even *think* about advice anymore tonight. I quickly typed back to Hailey.

So sorry. Bummer. Will discuss first thing in a.m. I promise! Hitting the hay. See you tomorrow.

Then I hurried to shut off my computer and get ready for bed.

Chapter 4

JOURNALIST SUCCESS AT TOP-SECRET ASSIGNMENT!

★ ★ ★

I had an e-mail from Michael when I woke up the next morning.

> Pasty,
> Let's meet at lunch to discuss lunch (the article. Get it?).
> ML

That was a great way to start the day, I must say!—with an invitation to lunch from your major crush. Even if he does call you by your horrible kindergarten nickname.

I decided to look at everything through rose-colored glasses. Tired of Waiting had gotten everything off her chest and, I'm sure, was now moving on, as I should.

Humming, I went online and skimmed the *New York Times* website, along with CNN, *Time* magazine, the Huffington Post, and the Daily Beast. I am pretty good at knowing which articles I should read and which I should skip. It's hard though. Sometimes I'll skip one, and then my social studies teacher brings up that topic that very day, and I feel like a dunce.

An IM popped up from Hailey.

Meet me @ locker. B early.

I looked at the clock and saw that if I left now, I could meet Hailey before homeroom.

At school I found Hailey waiting for me with a dramatic look on her face.

"Okay. Why do you think he likes someone else?" I asked immediately.

"Shh!" She looked around and then stared angrily at me. "Someone might hear you!" she hissed.

I looked around. There was almost no one there yet, and the people who *were* there were far away and very busy. No one could hear us. And anyway, how would they know who on Earth we were talking about?

"So you think he likes someone else?" I whispered.

Hailey nodded miserably.

"Why?" I asked.

She pouted. "I saw him leaving school with Amanda Huxtable yesterday. She's older. An eighth grader!"

Oh no. This was not good.

"That doesn't mean she's his girlfriend, silly!"

"It doesn't mean she's his mom, either!" Hailey's eyes flashed.

"Well, does he have any idea how much you like him?" I asked. Based on my own not-extensive experience, I know you can sometimes think someone knows you like them, but it turns out they don't know at all.

Hailey shook her head. "No."

"Are you sure?" I asked.

She shook her head harder. "I'm positive."

"Wait, when you talk to him, do you flirt or what?" I asked.

Hailey looked away. "I've never talked to him. I don't even know if he knows my name!"

"Whaaaat?! Hails, how do you even know if you like him, then?"

She met my eyes. "He's really cute and he's really good at soccer. He seems nice." She shrugged.

"And that's all it takes?" I asked.

She shrugged again. "I don't know. I guess. I've never really had a crush before, except kind of on Michael. And *you* picked him."

I took a deep breath to keep from strangling her. Then I tried hard to remember my mom's advice about *giving* advice. *Let people work through their own process. But don't give advice that you wouldn't take yourself.* I started slowly, not wanting to blurt out anything I couldn't take back. "Okay, first of all, you need to find out if Amanda Huxtable is really his girlfriend. Then, if not, and he is unattached, then . . . you need to actually speak with him before this goes any further. He might be a total nerd!"

"How am I supposed to speak with him?" she wailed.

I pressed my lips together, and thought hard. After a few seconds I had an aha moment! "Can you ask your coach to do a boys' and girls' varsity soccer practice together?"

Hailey looked at me in shock and then her whole face lit up. "You're a genius! I love you! You always give the best advice! I'm telling you, next year, they'd better make you Dear Know-It-All or else they're going to hear from me!" She gave me a huge hug and then trotted off happily.

Well, maybe I'm not totally terrible at this advice stuff!

I gathered my books and then headed off to class. As I passed the *Cherry Valley Voice* office, I happily poked in my head, feeling confident about helping Hailey and armed with my mom's new advice. There wasn't anyone in there, so I hopped onto the computer farthest from the door and went onto the server to see what had come in for Dear Know-It-All. Unfortunately, there was only one e-mail, and it was about school lunch and "Why can't they make it better?" Well, at least I was on the right track with that!

I logged out and quickly crossed the room, locking the office door so no one could go in. I whipped out Trigger's taxi keychain and hastily opened the Dear Know-It-All mailbox, grabbed a letter from inside, and slammed it shut, relocking it. Then I darted out into the hall, wedging the letter down into my messenger bag. My heart was pumping hard. I guess now I could see why Trigger thought of all this as spyish. I felt like James Bond completing a mission. I couldn't imagine *not* getting caught, especially getting the letters out of the mailbox, so it felt like a major victory. Phew. ***Journalist Success at Top-Secret Assignment!***

The only bummer was, after all that, I wouldn't be able to mention the lunch letter to Michael at our lunch about lunch! Ugh!

"Okay, what do we know?"

Michael looked distractingly adorable in his

long-sleeved turquoise T-shirt. His eyes reflected the shirt's color, and his dark skin and hair looked amazing against the brightness of his shirt.

"Hmm?" I asked, caught daydreaming about going on a date with him to the movies and holding hands.

Michael snapped his fingers. "Hello? Earth to Pasty! Let's hear back that list of what we know about school lunch."

"Right." The word "Pasty" snapped me right out of it. I began to read back what we'd brainstormed. "Gross food, unhealthy choices, bad ingredients, sits out too long." I looked at Michael after I finished. He was biting his lip in this cute way he has when he thinks hard.

"Okay. So what are our next steps?"

I read down the other list we'd compiled. "We need to interview the chef; get some man-on-the-street interviews from kids, kitchen staff, teachers, and parents; do a kitchen visit; maybe speak to Mr. Pfeiffer." I winced, and so did Michael. The principal didn't like us much after the last article we did about the new curriculum, but so be it. That was journalism for you. "If you make all the people happy all the time, then you're not doing your job," Trigger always says.

"Good. Let's divvy it up."

We split the assignments and agreed to see the school chef and kitchen staff together, and then Mr. Pfeiffer, and then our kitchen visit. Then we'd pool all our facts and come up with a thesis for the story. That's how we worked last time, and it came out really well.

"Look, I'm not worried about Pfeiffer. The whole article is going to be really light and easy. I mean, school food is gross. It's not exactly new news, right?"

"Yeah. We'll make it funny, too. I'm still thinking of a headline, like. . . 'Mac 'n' Queasy!' or something," Michael said with a mischievous grin.

"Yeah, or we could do a questionnaire format, like a survey piece: What do people hate the most? What's the grossest thing they've ever eaten in the cafeteria? Most fattening? Most unidentifiable?"

We were having fun. We laughed for a minute, but then I spotted Hailey across the room, giving me the thumbs-up sign with a big smile on her face. I gave her the thumbs-up back, but then she crooked her finger, beckoning me over. Ugh. Now I wished I hadn't seen her. Was it too late to pretend I had? I didn't want to leave Michael and the rosy glow of coauthorship.

But Hailey was now waving me over impatiently, using her whole arm. I sighed.

"You know what? I need to run," I said. "Sorry."

Michael turned to follow my gaze over his shoulder. He saw Hailey, and nodded. "Got it. Okay. Well, maybe you can interview her since it was her idea."

"Great. Bye," I said. Leaving gorgeous Michael Lawrence alone at a table felt like a crime, but duty called.

"What's up?" I asked Hailey when I reached her.

"The coaches said yes! You're a genius! They thought it was a brilliant idea, and we're doing it tomorrow! Thank you, Sammy!"

I smiled. "Great. Let me know how it goes."

"Oh no, you're coming to watch. I need your feedback on my interaction with Scott. You *can* come, can't you? Please? Please?" Hailey whined. She knows it drives me crazy when she whines and that I'll do anything to shut her up.

"Fine! Stop whining!" I could always do my homework while I watched from the bleachers. "But then you owe me an interview, okay?"

"Fine. About what? Soccer stardom? Romance?" Hailey fluffed her blonde hair with her fingers until it stuck up all over her head.

"School lunch."

"Yuck. Fine. After practice tomorrow at your house."

"Thanks. See ya." I had to go to the bathroom and I wanted to use it as my excuse to read my new letter from the Know-It-All mailbox. This day was going so well, there had to be a fabulous new question for the next issue.

In the girls' room, I used the bathroom and washed my hands, then ducked back into a stall to open the letter.

There was no return address, and despite the fact that the note writer was obviously in a real rush, I recognized the handwriting immediately this time.

Dear Knows Zero,

Your advice ruined my life.
I hate you.

From,

Tired of EVERYONE

Oh no! I sank down onto the toilet seat, fully clothed, and pressed my forehead against the cool metal of the stall. What now?

Chapter 5

RADAR STILL WORKING FOR LAME-O JOURNALIST

★ ★ ★

That night I watched TV. I couldn't deal with anything else. I finished my homework, got right in my pjs, and snuggled up on the couch with my mom to watch some bad reality show. I needed a major distraction. I just pushed everything out of my mind and forgot about it for a little while. I knew my mom was watching *me* out of the corners of her eyes, but she didn't press me, and I didn't offer any information, so we just let it ride.

At bedtime I didn't even check my computer. Well, only for a minute, to see if Michael had e-mailed anything important. Which he had!

Paste,
Interview with chef, kitchen staff,
Thurs. @ around 3 p.m. R u in?
ML

I replied yes, then went to bed.

My first thought the next morning was that I couldn't wait until Mr. Trigg came back. Only two more days. I decided then and there that I wouldn't check the Know-It-All letter box again while he was away, since Tired was sure to have written me another letter. (At least she wasn't an e-mailer!) I would just let him handle it when he returned, and if I didn't find an e-mail I liked on the server, the next column would have to wait.

Being decisive was a good way to start the day. I felt brisk and efficient while I read my news sites and blogs.

At school I zoomed through my classes, ate a roll and a bag of potato chips for lunch (giving me more great material for the gross lunch article), and was actually pleased to spend an hour outdoors supervising Hailey's love life since the weather was nice and my homework didn't require a computer. Hailey had been unable to find out if Amanda was Scott's girlfriend, so we were just proceeding with our Getting to Know Him plan.

I settled onto the bleachers, the sun warm on my back, and I pulled out my reading for language arts. The two teams spilled out onto the field, and I saw that Hailey noticed me, and nodded. I nodded back, feeling more like a spy every minute.

I am not a huge sports fan, so it was kind of boring for me to watch drills, but I quickly identified Scott and watched him like a hawk in between gulping down paragraphs of my language arts assignment. At one point the coaches pitted the captains against each other and the assistant captains against each other (Scott and Hailey were assistants). I watched her smile at him and say something funny, but he looked nervous and didn't really react.

Come on, Scott! I wanted to yell. *Give the girl a break!*

After another little while, the teams took a

break and ate the snacks they'd brought from home. Scott ended up next to Hailey, and she said something else to him, laughing, and for the second time, he didn't really react. Ugh! This was so annoying! It was painful to watch, actually. I wanted Hailey to succeed, and she was certainly trying, but Scott was frozen. Poor Hails. Was he shy? Or did he just not like her? Hard to tell.

As the practice ended, a few other people appeared on the bleachers. Baseball practice was up next, and they must've come to watch. I would have liked to stay myself and watch Michael in those cute little pants of his, but I really didn't have time. Soccer was wrapping up, and the boys' and girls' teams were doing a handshake line. As Scott passed Hailey, she smiled and then said something to him. This time he replied, but then he just smiled quickly and moved past her. It was a bummer. As he walked off the field, a girl who must've been Amanda Huxtable hopped off the bleachers and jogged over to him, and the two of them walked away. Okay, definitely his girlfriend. I decided to take it easy on Hailey.

I clanked my way down the bleachers, like an ill-timed oaf, stumbling on the last one, and jogged over to Hailey. She was gathering up her snack pouch and had a defeated air about her.

"Did the boys beat you?" I asked, trying to keep it light.

She looked at me, but didn't say anything.

"How did it go?" I asked, serious now.

"He's not that nice," she said.

I hadn't prepared what to say. "What do you mean?" I asked, pretending I couldn't tell that from a mile away.

"I tried to talk to him a little, and he was just really . . . unfriendly. Like, he didn't smile or really try to have a conversation or anything. At the end it seemed like he was warming up, but then Amanda Huxtable was here again. . . ." She gestured in the direction toward where Scott and the girl had walked. Aha! So I'd been right. Not that I was glad about it, but still. *Radar Still Working for Lame-o Journalist.*

"Maybe he's just not Mr. Personality," I suggested.

"He talks to the boys and jokes around with them!" She had started trudging up the hill to the front of the school. I followed, talking all the way.

"Maybe he's just shy around girls!"

"He's not shy around Amanda Huxtable," she said quietly. She turned to face me. "Tell me the truth. Will a boy ever like me?"

"Oh, Hailey! Of course! Lots of boys. You will have a lifetime of admirers, I promise! What about Jeff Perry?" I know he's interested in Hailey, and if she'd only like him back—It would be so convenient! We could double date, if Michael and I ever end up dating! But Hailey is not into him.

"Stop with Jeff Perry! *Please!* Okay, I guess you're right about Scott. I need some time to get to know him. Some time when Amanda Huxtable isn't around," she said darkly.

"Yeah, but just play it cool. Don't come on too strong, you know? He might be kind of shy, so go slow. Pretty soon you'll have him eating out of your hand."

"Right," she said. "As soon as Amanda's out of the picture."

"If she's actually in the picture."

"Right. Anyway, we've been talking about me all the time, and I don't even know what's going on with you. Anything up in the world of tabloid journalism?" We were out on the street now, walking slowly to Buttermilk Lane. The late afternoon sunlight fell in long shafts between the trees, and there were little mounds of dry leaves scattered everywhere.

"Oh, nothing." I waved my hand in dismissal. It wasn't like I could tell her. *Oh yeah, I'm being stalked by a crazy person who I gave bad advice to, under the guise of an anonymous column that you don't know I write.* Instead I said, "Working on the lunch article, which I need to interview you for when we get home. In love with Mikey as usual. Hating Allie as usual. All status quo." I crossed my toes as I lied to my best friend.

Hailey squinted at me, but I kept my face neutral. Luckily she was not a news hound like Allie. She let it go. *Antennae Broken, Friend Misses Signals for Help.*

At home we raided my kitchen and made a huge (junky) snack and then I interviewed Hailey.

"Okay, tell me what you think about the cafeteria food," I began, my pen poised above my trusty notebook on the kitchen table.

Hailey looked at the ceiling while she thought. "Well . . . there's not a lot I like to eat. Most days, I usually find just one little thing."

I pressed on. "Okay, like, what kinds of things do you like, when they have them?"

"Um, rice . . . with butter and salt. Rice Krispies Treats. JELL-O. Glazed doughnuts. French bread pizzas . . . That's kind of it."

"Wow," I said. Journalists aren't supposed to make value judgments about what their subjects tell them, usually, but it was hard to restrain myself. "Aren't you worried about cholesterol?" I teased. Hailey's mom was always yelling about not getting high cholesterol. Hailey made a face. "Seriously, though. If you could improve the food, what would you ask for?" I said.

"Easy!" said Hailey. "Either better, recognizable food, like the kind my mom would buy in the store, or something like Pizza Hut or McDonald's."

"O-kay . . ." I was getting it all down. "Interesting. Not sure others would say the same, but okay. And if you had one piece of advice for the chef, what would it be?"

Hailey laughed. "Go home!"

"I don't know if we can print that."

"Is that it?"

"For now. I might call you to follow up with a few more questions, once we have our thesis."

We went up to my room to do our language arts homework (Hailey always likes my help because she's dyslexic and she hates reading), and I left all my newspaper cares behind for a while.

We spent some time on Buddybook after we finished, and we found a treasure trove of Scott Parker photos from soccer on Jeff's sports page. I was happy for Hailey. It was fun to have a crush. It gave you focus. You just had to remember to keep everything in perspective. Unlike poor, crazy Tired, who was now actually really worrying me.

Chapter 6

JOURNALISTS AT WAR!

It was Thursday, the day of our interview with the kitchen staff. Michael and I didn't have a lot of prep work to do for this one because the questions were kind of simple. We were going to ask the cafeteria people point-blank why the food had to be so gross, and they were going to tell us. That was pretty much it.

Michael and I met in the hall at 2:50 p.m. as planned. He looked adorable in a white polo shirt and jeans—fresh and clean and classic. I had dressed up a little too—in a long hippie skirt and a pink T-shirt, with a scarf and dangly earrings—and the first thing Michael said was, "You look nice!"

I know I blushed, and I wasn't sure how to respond because it caught me off guard. I'm so used to him teasing me that my first instinct was to say something sarcastic back.

"Just say thanks, Pasty," he said, and the nickname allowed me to whomp him gently with my messenger bag and then the tension was broken. However, I made a mental note to make a bigger effort more often when choosing my clothes (or ask Allie for help) and also to try to pay him compliments too. Plus, it felt good to be on the receiving end.

I changed the subject. "So we're just going to go with the flow, right? Keep it loose and see what they say?"

Michael nodded. "I don't have an agenda. We'll probably have to do a follow-up once we have our thesis, anyway."

I nodded, and we entered the cafeteria. Sitting at a far table were three grown-ups, each dressed in kitchen whites and each holding a cup of coffee or tea. I recognized them all but realized with a pang of guilt that after more than a year at this school, I didn't know any of their names.

Michael strode ahead confidently, and when he reached them, he introduced himself and shook hands all around. I followed suit, feeling shy. There was one man and two women. I wondered which one was the chef, but didn't have to wonder long.

"Mary couldn't be here. She says sorry. She had to go to a meeting with the superintendent of schools," said one of the ladies whose name was Marcy. She had a raspy voice and thick blond hair in a braid and covered by a black hairnet. She looked about the age of a lot of moms.

"The meetings never end! I would not want that job," said the other woman, Carmen, who was younger. Her hair was short, dark, and curly, but matted down under the hairnet. I wondered why they kept the nets on when they weren't in the kitchen.

"Pay's better," said the guy, who had a big blond mustache and also a long blond braid of hair under his hairnet. His name was Bob, and he had tattoos up his arms and a little on his neck. He looked like he should be driving a Harley-Davidson motorcycle.

I could tell that Michael felt things drifting out of our control. He cleared his throat. "Thanks for meeting us today. We are doing an article for the *Cherry Valley Voice* on school lunches. . . ."

"What's the *Cherry Valley Voice?*" asked Carmen.

"Uh . . . the school newspaper?" said Michael, and we looked at each other. We were both surprised she didn't know. She must've been new.

Carmen nodded, and Michael continued. "We want to learn a little about how you guys decide what to make and why it's . . ." Now that we were face to face with these people who worked hard to feed us every day, it was difficult to be aggressive.

"Why it isn't so tasty all the time," I said in what I hoped was tactful phrasing.

Bob rolled his eyes, and Marcy leaned back in her seat. "I get it," she said. "We're the bad guys in this article, right?"

Michael cocked his head. I guess this wasn't going to go as smoothly as we had expected. "No, there are no bad guys," he said. "We know you're doing your jobs here, and that it's not easy."

"Not easy!" said Marcy. "It's darn near impossible! We've got bureaucracy coming out of our ears! Every time Mary wants to try something new, they just shut her down. And the restrictions and regulations!"

Bob shook his head. "Phew!" he said. I guess he was a man of few words.

Carmen was nodding. "Mary's gotta plan out a menu a year in advance and have it approved by April so the central ordering can start. It's a lot of work."

"We're understaffed," said Bob.

"The food needs to be healthy, and it can't be imported. There are standards of how much of each food group each kid needs to get each day, plus portion control," explained Carmen.

"We're not allowed to give big portions 'cause kids are getting obese," said Marcy. Michael and I exchanged a glance.

"What are some other issues you're dealing with?" Michael asked quietly. We were on the retreat now instead of the attack. My hand was already sore from taking notes.

Marcy started ticking things off on her fingers. "Gotta make three meals a day. Lunch is our biggest meal, but we also serve breakfast and an after-school snack to kids who need extra help. This might be all the food they get for the day. That's not a problem you two have, I can see, but there's more of them than you might know."

Marcy continued. "We need to look out for allergens—no nuts, no shellfish in the main course—so that knocks out a lot of possible protein sources for us. Food needs to be cooked to a certain temperature and kept there because of E. coli and mad cow disease, so a lot of the food dries out. Those last two are per the department of health and human services. Oh, and the budgets were all cut this year. We have no money."

"Also we have to triple wash produce, so we can't serve anything fragile, like berries or fancy lettuce, 'cause they don't hold up. You wash it hard three times, and it falls apart or gets bruised. So it's mostly iceberg and bananas or apples," said Carmen.

Oh boy, I thought. *Serving lunch food that wasn't*

gross was a lot harder than we thought.

"How long have you been working here?" asked Michael.

"Eighteen years," said Marcy.

"Twelve," said Bob.

"Sixteen," added Carmen.

And none of them knew the name of the school paper! I think my jaw actually dropped.

"So you must like it here, then?" asked Michael.

"Mary's great to work for," said Carmen with a smile. "She really loves food, and she makes it fun."

"Wow. I'm looking forward to meeting her," I said.

"So what do you hear from the kids?" asked Carmen. "Is there anything they like?"

I laughed. "The junk."

Marcy shook her head sadly.

"That's kids for ya," said Bob.

"Is there anything you can do to make the food . . . I don't know . . ." I didn't want to say "better" because it seemed mean.

"Better?" said Bob, echoing my thoughts.

I laughed. "Yeah."

Marcy spoke up. "Mary has piles of good ideas.

It's just hard to develop 'em and get 'em approved."

"Takes lots of time," agreed Bob.

"And with the budget cuts . . ." Carmen added.

I looked at the three of them. "You guys are dealing with a lot. I have a whole new appreciation for what you're up against and what you're trying to accomplish."

Marcy shrugged. "It's what we do," she said.

"Four thousand meals a week, counting the one hundred breakfasts and after-school snacks each day." Carmen nodded with a wry smile.

I put my forehead in my hand. "And there're only four of you?" I muttered.

Michael stood, ready to wrap it up. We were heading into complaining territory, and he always has a nose for when the news is done and the repetitive complaining takes over. "I have to go to practice, so we're going to have to go now. Thank you so much for your time and your thoughts," he said.

I stood and shook hands with Marcy, Carmen, and Bob. "We'll come find Mary another time," I said. "And we'll probably have more questions for you once we shape up the article. I'll be in touch if we need a second interview."

"Thanks for coming," said Bob. "It's the first time any of you kids ever talked to us, except to ask for seconds." He laughed.

"Bye!" Michael and I said in unison.

Out in the hall, I slumped against the wall. "Are you kidding me with that? I feel terrible now that I know what they're up against," I said to Michael.

He nodded. "It's crazy. But it's still not an excuse for bad food," he added.

"That's pretty harsh," I said.

He shrugged. "I don't know. You've got to stay objective."

"I'd love to hear *your* thoughts on how they could improve it," I said. I knew I was being a little testy, but why did he have to be so mean about the poor cafeteria people? At least they were trying!

"I'd love to hear Mary's," Michael said, "but she blew us off."

"Is that what you think?" I asked.

"You never know," he said.

"Wow. That's a pretty negative attitude."

"I'm just saying you never know. You've got to keep your antennae up at all times, Sam. Don't let your emotions get the best of you."

Ha! Me? Emotions? I'm all about facts. I'm all about being objective!

Michael looked at me, like he was going to say something else, but then he decided not to. "Look, journalists are there to report, not to get involved."

I set my jaw firmly. "That's not necessarily true. Journalists get involved all the time. And then they print stories that make change happen."

Michael looked at me for an extra second. "I've gotta go," he said.

"Bye," I said, looking away. *Journalists at War!*

Were we in a fight? I wondered as I walked away. It felt weird. I was annoyed at him for being uncaring, but a tiny part of me *did* worry that he was a better reporter than me. Michael was right. I shouldn't have let myself feel sorry for the cafeteria workers. And now I was mad because I was embarrassed at being caught making a rookie mistake. But how are you going to write about things if you can't feel them yourself? I know journalists need to remain objective, but they need to care, too. It's a really hard balance to keep.

I thought of Tired, and that maybe I was caring too much about her mean notes. Maybe it was time for me to toughen up and take charge! Why hide from my responsibilities, just because I was scared off by the rantings of some nut job? Journalists get letters from kooks all the time!

The *Cherry Valley Voice* office is usually empty at that time of day. I took a left and strode down the hall toward the office. My heels struck the floor hard, and rang in the emptiness. I was trying to be brave. But as I drew closer to the office, I decided I'd only check e-mails. (Yes, I knew Tired only wrote letters but still. It was a start!)

At the office, I unlocked the door, took a quick look around, and seeing no one there, I went to the computer that was farthest away, and logged into the server, then I accessed the Know-It-All file with my password. "Bring it on, Tired," I muttered, confident I'd find nothing.

The computers are slow in the *Cherry Valley Voice* office, so I gazed at the posters on the newsroom wall while I waited for the e-mails to load. Like the one in Mr. Trigg's office, these were mostly British World War II posters ("Loose Lips Sink Ships!" and "Keep Calm and Carry On"). They were kind of inspiring.

Feeling brave, I glanced back at the screen to see if it had loaded, and I gasped.

There were forty-two new e-mails in the file.

And they were all from Tired.

Chapter 7

IMPARTIALITY IMPOSSIBLE FOR JUVENILE JOURNALIST

★ ★ ★

I could feel myself turning bright red—whether from embarrassment or fear or anger, or a combination of all three, I wasn't sure. I just knew I couldn't breathe. All my bravery and objectiveness had evaporated.

My hands shook as I clicked on the first e-mail, starting from the bottom.

Why are you Know-It-All, anyway? You're probably ugly and stupid, and no one likes you.

I cringed. Nervously I clicked on the next e-mail. The next one said:

YOU ARE A FAILURE!!!!!!!!!!!!!!!!!!!!!!!!!!!

And the next one:

I hate you, Know-It-All. You ruined
my life!!!!!!!!!!!!!!!!!!!!!!

Tears pricked my eyes. My hands were shaking
so badly, I had to fold them together. I had ruined
someone's life with my dumb advice! I thought I
was so snappy and clever, and look what I did! Now
this person, Tired, was coming totally unglued.
I wanted to read all of the e-mails, but I was too
scared. If these were the first three, I could only
imagine what number forty-two looked like. Part of
me wanted to read them, just to punish myself, but
the rational part of my brain knew that this person
had gone crazy. and I should keep away.

Tears poured out of my eyes as I shut the computer down, locked up the office, and then fled
the *Voice* office. I wiped my face on my sleeve and
prayed I wouldn't run into anyone. I had almost

reached the front door of the school when I saw someone ahead of me, and it was too late for me to turn away and hide. It was an adult, with long blond hair in a braid. Marcy, from the cafeteria.

Oh my gosh, I wanted to die. I blotted my eyes on my sleeve again, just as she turned to see who was coming up behind her.

"Hey, honey," she said with a smile, but her friendly expression quickly changed to one of concern. "What's the matter, baby? Are you all right?"

I nodded, my lips pressed into a fake smile, but tears were streaming down my face again. I never, ever cry, but every once in a while, it all comes out, and then I can't stop. I could already tell that this was going to be one of those times.

Marcy was looking closely at me, with a worried frown on her face. "Can I help you? Is there anything you need?" She bent down and put a comforting hand on my shoulder.

I shook my head, still trying to smile through my tears. "I'm . . . okay . . . It's just . . . dumb," I said, trying not to sob.

"Oh, honey." She reached into her purse, pulled out a packet of Kleenex, and handed me a wad of them. I mopped my eyes and took big, ragged breaths.

"Here," she offered me a mint, and I took that, too.

"Thanks," I croaked.

"Would you like me to call someone for you? Do you need a ride?"

I shook my head no. "I'm fine," I said.

Marcy laughed a little. "You don't look fine!"

I laughed a little too, and then gulped. "It's just one of those things."

Marcy bit her lip thoughtfully. "I wouldn't want to be your age again for all the tea in China," she said. "Things are rough in middle school. I see it all the time in the cafeteria. Kids don't notice us. We're invisible. So we see people doing things—being mean to other kids, bullying, falling in love, breaking up. It's hard going through all that stuff, especially for the first time."

I nodded and took a deep breath. My tears were under control now. As long as I didn't think about the e-mails from Tired, I could be okay. I could make it home.

"Okay now, honey?" Marcy tilted her head and looked at me. She was obviously a mom.

"Yes," I said with a big sigh.

She reached out and patted me on the head. "It gets easier. I promise," she said with a smile. "And hey, I have good news! Mary called. She's putting a suggestion box in the cafeteria tomorrow!"

I managed a smile. "Great! Thanks!"

"All right now, I'm off. Feel better, okay?"

"Thanks, Marcy."

We walked out into the late afternoon sunshine. It was chilly, and that made me feel better. I wished I had sunglasses to hide my red eyes.

"See you tomorrow!' Marcy called, and she walked toward her car.

I waved. So much for not getting emotionally involved with your subjects. Michael would have a fit if he knew I'd been practically sobbing at school on Marcy's shoulder. *Impartiality Impossible for Juvenile Journalist.*

All the way home—it's six blocks to 17 Buttermilk Lane—I speed-walked, singing a dumb Katy Perry song in my head to keep pace. Anything, just so I didn't have to think.

At home I opened the door, ran upstairs, and threw myself onto my bed, where I sobbed for fifteen minutes. Between arguing with Michael and the e-mails from Tired, it was the worst day ever. So what did I do?

I fell sound asleep.

I woke up an hour later to the smell of melted chocolate wafting into my room. It smelled delicious, and I realized I was starving. I went into the bathroom and splashed cold water on my face and then I headed downstairs to see what was cooking.

In the kitchen Allie was standing by the oven, wearing pot holders and an apron. She was holding a sheet pan with something on it. Allie wasn't exactly a cook. And she didn't generally operate appliances that didn't text her back. What was going on?

"Yum!" I said.

Allie jumped. "I didn't know you were home!"

"I fell asleep," I said.

"Why?" Allie asked. She turned and looked at me carefully. "Hey, were you crying?"

It would be hard to flat-out lie, so I just fibbed. "A little. It's nothing." I shrugged. "What are you making?" I crossed the kitchen to take a look.

"It's one of those Mrs. Moseby recipes you recommended. I decided to sample a few before I bothered posting it on the website. Is it something about Michael Lawrence?" The girl did not give up, ever.

As if! I thought angrily. But I wasn't going to let Allie know that. "No . . . it's nothing."

She looked at me suspiciously. "Are you sure you don't want me to talk to Will or Tommy about your crush? I know they'd be willing to put in a good word." Allie really loved lording it over me that she knew Michael's older brothers. Like she had all the power in my love life.

"No! Do *not* talk to them. If you do, I will tell Mom, and you'll get in trouble!"

"Fine! Sheesh. Can't blame a girl for trying!"

"Speaking of trying, can I try one of those things you're making? What are they, anyway?"

"It's rolled oats with molasses and dark-chocolate chunks. You can also add almonds or dried cherries or seeds or whatever, but we don't have any of that stuff."

Allie cut me a slice, and I blew on it then took a bite. It was delicious! Chewy, not too sweet, a little crunchy, and good for you. "Yum!" I said. It was really tasty. Maybe I could start bringing these to school so I wouldn't need to take charity granola bars from stupid Michael Lawrence.

Allie had cut her own slice, and was chewing thoughtfully. "Pretty good," she agreed.

"What other recipes does she have?"

"Fruit skewers, whole-wheat pretzel clusters, frozen bananas rolled in peanut butter and raisins, yogurt pops, smoothies, cereal bars . . ."

"And there are meal recipes on there, too, right?"

Allie nodded. "Yeah. We should show Mom. We could make some of the stuff for dinner." She put down her plate, took her phone out of her apron pocket (of course), and began to text.

"What are you texting?" I asked.

"Just texting about Mrs. Moseby. People should check her out."

"How many Buddybook friends do you have?" I asked.

Allie shrugged. "Six hundred."

"Six hundred?!" That was an astounding number to me. I couldn't imagine six hundred people being interested in what I had to say. *Especially because I'm usually wrong*, I thought morosely, the Tired e-mails washing back over me in a wave. Mr. Trigg would be back tomorrow. I couldn't wait. "Don't you worry you'll text something that's . . . wrong?" I asked.

Allie shrugged again. "Not really. It's just my opinion. And hey, at least I'm putting it out there. I'm trying, you know? If people don't like it, they don't have to keep reading. They can stop following you."

"Huh," I said, wishing I had her confidence. I guess people don't *have* to read Dear Know-It-All's answers. Or they don't *have* to do what Dear

Know-It-All tells them to do if they don't want to. I shuddered a little and then stood up. It was time to start my homework. "Thanks for the snack," I said.

"Anytime," said Allie. "And think about my offer."

"What offer?" I was confused.

"To tell the Lawrence boys about your love."

"Oh please! Never!"

The weekend passed in a blur of homework and errands with my mom. Hailey slept over Saturday night, and we went to the movies on Sunday and then came up for a few ways for her to try to talk to Scott. It was a pretty mellow weekend. Sunday night, I had an IM from Hailey.

Huxtable not his girlfriend!!!!!!!!!!
What now?

What now, indeed, I thought. I sighed. Some-times Know-It-All doesn't know.

Chapter 8

GIRL DIES OF SHOCK IN SCHOOL KITCHEN. A FEW PEOPLE MOURN.

★ ★ ★

Hailey was waiting for me at my locker the next morning, naturally, a huge smile on her face.

"So?" she asked, launching right in.

"I think it's great news!" I said.

"I know, I know," Hailey agreed, nodding and smiling modestly. "So, really. What now?"

"Um, get to know him?"

"I knew you were going to say that!" Hailey groaned. "But how?"

"Well, more coed soccer practices? Or find out what else he does?" This was where my advice fell apart. I knew you could share interests and activities with your crush, but it didn't mean he'd end up liking you. *Or that you'd like* him, I thought.

By now, my anger at Michael had faded to being just annoyed, and most of it was at myself, I had to say. I knew he was right about remaining objective, and it ticked me off that I wasn't as good at it as he was. He was right to call me on it.

Suddenly I felt myself swept off my feet and spun into the air. I kind of lost my breath. When I was set back down on my feet, I turned around to confront my spinner, and I saw that it was Michael himself, a huge, sooooo-cute grin on his face. He looked gorgeous, his eyes flashing happily, and his cheeks a little pink. I hope they weren't pink from lifting me up. I was almost as tall as him.

He launched right in. "Sorry about yesterday, Pasty. I shouldn't have been so self-righteous. Great news, though! Mary the chef e-mailed me to apologize for bailing yesterday and to ask for a meeting today after school!"

How could I stay mad? I grinned back. "Apology accepted on the condition that you never talk down to me, your coreporter, like that again." I put my hands on my hips.

"Deal," said Michael, and he put out his big

warm hand for me to shake.

I wished I could hold onto his hand forever. "So that's great news about Mary. What time?"

"Right after school."

Darn. That was when I had planned to chat with Trigger, now that he was back. I sighed. I guess one more day wouldn't kill me. "Fine," I said.

"Don't look so excited!" Michael teased.

"No, I'm excited. Thanks. That's great."

Michael looked at Hailey. "What's gotten into this one?" he asked, jerking a thumb at me.

Hailey shook her head. "She's a mystery even to me," she said.

"Shut up, you two," I said, smiling. They'd made me laugh. "I'll see you at the meeting. I've gotta run to Earthonomics, or whatever our science class is called now."

Right after school I met Michael outside the cafeteria.

As a joke I chanted, "Objective, objective, objective," under my breath.

"Very funny," he said, and he swatted me as he swung open the door.

No one was in the cafeteria, so we wandered back into the kitchen, calling "Hel-looo!"

"In here!" called a friendly voice.

We turned a corner, and there was Mary Bonner, the chef. Seeing her now, I realized that I had seen her before, but never knew who she was. She wasn't wearing chef's clothes, but rather a pretty flowered dress with a crisp white apron over it. She had red hair and freckles and a smile with dimples, and she looked like one of those ladies you saw on a TV cooking show. She was not what I'd been expecting!

"Hi! Thanks for coming on such short notice!" she said. "I'm Mary Bonner, the executive chef here." She put out her hand, and Michael and I took turns shaking it and introducing ourselves.

"I've just been testing out a new recipe. It's lots of work, so I'm ready for a break. Let's sit over here." She led us to a round table with four chairs and a striped oilcloth table covering. It was cozy, like you'd find in someone's house.

"Would either of you like some tea?" she asked, gesturing to an electric teakettle that was steaming on the counter.

We said, "No thanks," and she put down a big plate of cookies in the middle of the table and joined us.

"Here, help yourself."

I looked at Michael. Was it objective if I had a cookie? They looked and smelled amazing. They had chocolate chips in them, but it looked like there was a bunch of other stuff, too.

"Go on! They're not poison! And I love to see kids eat!" Mary said, smiling warmly.

"Thanks," I said, and I picked one up and took a bite. It crunched, which surprised me, and it was salty and sweet and chewy, too. It was delicious!

My eyes nearly popped out of my head as I chewed.

"Wow! What is this? It's great! Michael, you've got to have one. Go ahead."

He took one and Mary laughed. "It's a compost cookie," she said. "It's basically a chocolate-chip cookie but you throw all kinds of leftovers into the batter, too, like pretzels or potato chips, mini-marshmallows—whatever you have lying around."

Amazing! Everyone would love these.

Compost Cookie Starts School Riots.

"Wow! I love it! Why can't we have these at lunch?" I asked without thinking, then I covered my hand with my mouth. I hadn't meant to be rude.

Mary laughed gently. She wasn't mad. "I wish!" she said. "The ingredients are just too expensive. And, for our baked goods we have to use mixes that come from a central plant."

"Why?" I asked.

"State law," said Mary sadly. She sighed. "So I know you have questions for me, but I'm excited to show you the suggestion box and the reaction we've had already, in only a day and a half!"

She stood and went to her desk, then she brought back a shoe box that was overflowing with notes. "Look at this!" she said happily. "Here, read some!"

I chose a piece of paper. It said, "The food stinks. Can't you do better?"

I was shocked. My jaw dropped, and I looked at Mary, but she was still smiling. I picked another.

"Lunch makes me puke . . . And why can't we have more cookies?"

One after another, I read them all; about seventy total. Different writing paper, different handwriting, all obviously from lots of different people. But they all pretty much said the same thing.

"Yikes," said Michael.

"Double yikes," I added. I looked at Mary. "Aren't your feelings hurt?" I asked her.

"Not at all! I'm thrilled!"

This woman was either a nut job or she knew something I didn't know. "Why?" I asked.

Mary rested her elbows on the table and put her chin on her hands. She looked really young, but I guessed she was about my mom's age. "For two reasons. One, I'm thrilled that kids care enough about the food to take the time to write a note. It shows how much the food matters to them and how much they think about it, which I've known all along. The second reason is that it reinforces what I've been telling everyone all along. The kids hate the food." She smiled again.

"But it's your food they hate!" I blurted.

Mary shook her head. "No, it's not. It's the government's food! It's what *they* say I have to make, with the ingredients they send me. Listen, we try the best we can to make it taste good. But our equipment in here is way behind the times—the warmers make everything mushy and the coolers make everything wilt—and the frozen stuff they send me is really gross, not to mention unhealthy. Or some of it at least. I have dozens of recipes and suppliers I'm dying to use, but they won't let me."

"Why?" Michael asked. I glanced at him. He was really into this, I could tell. He was getting all fired up. "Unions, trade agreements, vendor contracts, RDA quotas, public interest groups, lack of funds. It's a lot that we're up against. Look, I'm a trained chef. I've worked in fancy restaurants in the city and cute café's around here. I took this job because I liked the schedule—it let me have summers off to be with my kids—but I also took it because I thought I could make a difference. I had no idea how hard it would be to change anything!" She pounded her fist on the table. "So I want to put together a plan. I want to incorporate the suggestions of the kids, tweak them a little to keep them healthy, take a big proposal to the

principal and to the superintendent of schools—
all the way up—and I want to get things changed
around here. The suggestion box was a great start.
Marcy's idea, by the way." She winked at me. Oh
gosh, I guess she knew I'd been crying on Marcy's
shoulder. I glanced at Michael, feeling uncomfortable. I hoped Mary wouldn't say anything.

"Great!" said Michael. "I'm sure we can help
you," he added.

I looked at him. *What about not getting involved,
mister?* I wanted to say. Ha!

Mary was nodding. "Thanks," she said. And
then she looked wistful. "The one thing I'd just
love to have is a little garden, or a tiny greenhouse, where kids could help grow some fresh
organic herbs that we could incorporate into the
meals. You wouldn't believe how much success
they've had in California with this sort of thing.
Kids who grow food themselves are more likely to
try it multiple times and in multiple ways. They're
more likely to ask their parents to buy it at home.
Plus, fresh organic food is the healthiest choice.
And it's good for the planet!" Mary was glowing

with excitement. She laughed at herself. "Oh, here I am getting on my bandwagon again!"

Michael and I laughed. "No, it's great," I protested. "It's like what we're learning about in . . ." And I stopped, thunderstruck. "Hey! I just had an idea! You know how we have this new curriculum?"

Mary nodded. Michael was looking at me curiously.

"Well, in Earthonomics, which is like science, we learn about all this stuff—agriculture and business and health and the environment and whatever. Maybe we could incorporate something into the class about growing and harvesting our own food."

"Wonderful!" said Mary. I glanced nervously at Michael. Was I being objective enough for him? I was actually getting involved with the news!

But Michael had a pleased, kind of impressed expression on his face. He nodded. "Great idea, Paste—uh, Sam."

Now it was my turn to smile. Michael almost never calls me by my real name.

"We could do a series of articles," I suggested.

"One article about how bad lunch has been and the suggestion box. Then one about your plans and then a follow-up. What do you think?"

Mary was nodding. "I'll put together a proposal—I'll include something about Earthonomics and make sure to credit you, Sam—and I'll get a meeting with Mr. Pfeiffer. Maybe you two would like to come?"

Michael and I looked at each other and laughed as we stood to leave. I put my notebook and pen away in my bag. "Why don't you present it as your own idea first. Then see what he says. We'll report on it after that," I suggested.

Mary looked confused, but she let it go. "Great! And I'll go through the recipes on my blog and see what we can pull together for fresh herbs. It's a start!"

"Wait, you have a blog?" asked Michael.

Mary nodded. "Just with healthy recipes and stuff like that. Ideas."

I pulled my pen and notebook back out of my messenger bag. "What's it called?" I asked. I'd look it up and incorporate it into the article.

"Mrs. Moseby's Home Cooking," said Mary with a smile.

You could have knocked me over with a feather. I'd have to get Allie's stats on Mary's popularity at the high school and incorporate it into the article. This was just crazy! I was almost speechless. "You're Mrs. Moseby?" I sputtered. *Girl Dies of Shock in School Kitchen. A Few People Mourn.*

"But you're Mrs. *Bonner*," said Michael.

"Mrs. Moseby was my grandmother's name," said Mary. "It just had a certain charm to it, so I used it for my blog." She shrugged. "Thanks for coming, kids!"

Out in the hall I turned to Michael and laughed. "So much for objective journalism. Huh, pal?"

He just shook his head and laughed.

I had to think for a minute. Between the "be objective" issue with the school lunch article and the advice I'd given Tired, plus her backlash, I was so confused about my role as a journalist. Could you get excited about a story and still be objective? And did it make me less of a journalist if I cared what people thought about what I wrote? I wished I could talk to Michael about the

Tired problem, but it wasn't like I could exactly tell him. I thought for a minute. Maybe I could . . .

"You know, some days you think you're right, and it turns out you're wrong. And other days you think you're wrong, but it turns out you're right! So what do you do when you're wrong?"

Michael looked taken aback. "I know I was wrong. I'm sorry. I . . ."

"No, no, no, not you, silly. I was wrong about something. Really wrong. Now what do I do?"

Michael looked uncomfortable. "You've got a good head on your shoulders, Pasty. You always know what to do. I wouldn't . . . uh . . . worry about being wrong. Unless it's about someone else, who . . . "

Who what? What was he trying to say?

"Oh never mind. I've got football," he said, and he walked off.

"Bye!" I called. "Weirdo," I whispered. "And thanks for nothing."

Boys. Can't live with 'em, can't live . . . with 'em.

Chapter 9

COVER BLOWN, ANONYMOUS JOURNO MOVES TO SIBERIA

★ ★ ★

I practically ran home. I was dying to tell Allie about meeting Mrs. Moseby and what a coincidence the whole thing had been.

"Al-*leeeee!*" I yelled as I flung open the front door.

I could hear her chatting away in her room, probably on the phone.

"Al!" I yelled, taking the stairs two at a time. "Guess what?"

Out of habit I knocked on her door, even though it was open. I winced at myself for being so well trained. She was at her desk on the phone.

"Allie," I whispered hard.

She held one finger aloft, telling me to wait.

I sighed and stood in the doorway, tapping my foot. There was nothing to do but eavesdrop.

"Wow. Uh-huh. Crazy stuff! No, never when I was there. But then they didn't really have Buddybook then. Yeah. Well, my sister just walked in, and she goes there, so I'll ask. Okay, I'll call you back. Bye!"

Allie turned in her desk chair. "Oh my goodness! You'll never believe this!" she said dramatically.

Since most things are dramatic for Allie and her friends, I knew, by my standards, that it could probably wait. "No, mine is better, I'm sure. Guess what?" I grinned, sitting down on her bed.

Allie folded her arms across her chest, a smug look on her face. "Okay, but I am *positive* that mine is better. But whatever, by all means, you go first."

Ugh. Why does she have to torture me so? I refused to take the bait. "Fine, whatever. Guess who I met today?" I smiled and folded my arms as she had.

"Justin Bieber," she said with a bored inflection.

"No, better."

"Better than the Beebs? Impossible!" she scoffed.

"Come on, Allie! Be serious! It's someone you really like but don't know."

"Zac Efron?" she said with a smile.

I couldn't stand the teasing any longer. "Argh! Mrs. Moseby!" I blurted.

"Hey, random! That's pretty cool! Where?" At least Allie was reacting appropriately, even if she wasn't as excited as I thought she'd be.

"She is—drumroll, please—our school chef!" I was pretty pleased with myself as I delivered this news.

"What? No way! Then why does the food stink so much?" Allie asked.

"Well, funny you should mention it. We were interviewing her today, and it was supposed to be all about why is the food so bad, but it turned out—"

We were interrupted by the ringing of Allie's phone. So annoying! And of course she picked it right up.

"No!" she said to whomever. "I haven't had a chance to ask her yet! I will call you back when I find out." She hung up.

Was she talking about me?

"Wait, so what's your big news?" I asked.

Allie got all dramatic again and made her eyes go really wide. She sat forward in her chair and then said, "Do you know who Dear Know-It-All is this year at your school?"

What? My heart began to thump in my chest, and I instantly felt hot and sweaty. How did she find out?

"Wait, Allie, please—"

"Get a load of this!" she said, and she thrust her phone at me.

I looked at it, not comprehending. Then everything came into focus. There was a post on the wall of the high school's Buddybook page from someone called TiredofWaiting. It said: "Dear Know-It-All at Cherry Valley Middle School is a chicken and an idiot. Come out, come out, wherever you are!!!"

I froze. My heat had turned to an icy chill. This was scary.

"How did you get this?" I asked. I felt my heart starting to beat really fast, and my palms were sweaty. This had just taken things to a new level. A dangerous one.

Allie shrugged. "They wrote it on the school's Buddybook wall that I administer. Can you believe it? What did Know-It-All do? I don't follow middle school 'journalism.'" She made quotation marks in the air with her fingers to show just what she thought of our paper.

Even in the midst of a crisis, Allie found a way to be superior.

"Well, there was a column this week about a girl asking a boy out. She said, I mean, he or she said to do it."

"Huh," said Allie. "Well, that's not bad advice, but I guess it didn't go so well. Probably some dramatic kid overreacting. Definitely not as interesting as I thought. Nobody will care by tomorrow."

Right. As if.

I stood carefully and collected my messenger bag.

"Well, I guess I'll go start my homework now," I said casually.

"Listen, news hound, let me know if you hear anything. The poor kid who writes that column. He's really in for it! I wish I could be a fly on the wall!"

I turned to walk away, so she wouldn't see my

face. "I'll let you know. . . ."

Allie started texting away on her phone. "I'm going to text this post," she said. "Maybe one of my six hundred or so Buddybook friends has an idea who is Know-It-All."

"Allie, wait—" I began. But Allie already looked up with a pleased smile. "Done," she said.

I got to my room as fast as I could without looking suspicious. Then I quickly closed my door, sat down at my computer, and started to shake. I was shaking so hard, I couldn't even type to send an emergency e-mail to Trigger. I had to sit on my hands. Thoughts raced through my mind. Was Tired going to find me? Could she actually find out who I was if she wanted to? I didn't know what to do. All I knew was this: I did not want to be the Dear Know-It-All anymore.

Minutes passed, and I collected myself. How could I talk to Mr. Trigg without someone seeing me and guessing? Could I call him at home? But what if Allie heard me? I felt so alone.

And then I heard my mom come in. "Hi, girls!" she called.

Thank goodness!

"Hey, Mom!" Allie replied.

I paused for a minute, so I wouldn't make Allie think anything, then I stood and opened my door and crept down the stairs. In the kitchen, I tiptoed to find my mom.

"Mom!" I whispered.

"Ooh!" She jumped in the air and dropped the bread she was putting away from the grocery bag.

Despite myself I had to grin. "Sorry."

She leaned back against the counter and put her hand to her chest. Then she laughed. "Why so quiet?"

I spoke urgently, in a low voice, and my mom's smile faded as she listened. "Mom, a major emergency has come up with the paper. We can't let Allie know. Do you have Mr. Trigg's cell phone or address or anything by any chance?"

"I think so, but, honey, what is it? Can't I help you?" she asked quietly.

I shook my head. "I need the number and your cell phone and then I need to go on a walk and call him in private."

My mother looked at me suspiciously, hesitating.

"Please. I'll tell you everything after," I promised. My eyes were about to fill with tears, but I willed them away. If I cried she would definitely insist on getting involved right now.

She sighed heavily. "Fine, it's just down at my desk. I'll go get it. But I want to hear the whole story when you get back, okay?"

"What whole story?" asked Allie, coming into the kitchen. Darn it!

"Uh . . ." *Think, Martone! Think!* "Uh." I looked at her, then a stroke of pure genius hit me. I crossed my toes in my shoes, and began. "Michael Lawrence and I are in a fight. I don't know how to fix it. I'm going over there to make a stand. I'm going to tell him that I like him. That I've always liked him. So there!" I spoke like a heroine in a movie, adding a little toss of my hair at the end, just like I'd seen Allie do.

Allie's face looked like I'd just given her the best birthday present ever. Her jaw dropped and then she smiled a huge smile and reached out and hugged me! Then she held me away from her by the shoulders and said, "All right, sister! You go! Go get your man!" She swatted me on the butt in encouragement. Then she spun me around. "Is that what you're wearing?"

Just then my mother came back into the kitchen with her cell phone and a number.

Allie's eyes narrowed suspiciously. She looked back and forth between the two of us. "Wait . . ."

"Sheesh, Mom. It's not *that* far. I just couldn't remember the name of the street. I didn't need you to write it down for me!" I lied. I took the piece of paper from my (poor, innocent) mom and rolled my eyes at Allie. My mom was holding out her cell phone in the other hand. "What? And the phone too? Oh please!" I lied again, and I took that too. "Fine. I'll call you when I get there. Mothers," I said to Allie, shaking my head.

Her face relaxed into a smile. "I know," she said.

I didn't dare look at my mother, but instead headed out the door. Phew.

Once I was safely around the corner, I ducked

into a hedge and dialed Mr. Trigg's number.

"Hello?" he said.

"Mr. Trigg," I began. And then I started to cry.

Objectivity Fails When Journo Is Scared.

Chapter 10

JOURNALIST FLOODS NEIGHBORHOOD WITH RECORD TEAR FALL!

★ ★ ★

"I'm sorry, who is this?" Mr. Trigg's voice was patient and kind, and that made me cry harder. Wow, three times in one week. That was a new record for me. Usually I only cry about once every other month! *Journalist Floods Neighborhood with Record Tear Fall!*

I hiccupped and tried again. "Mr. Trigg, it's—" But the crying got me again. Now I was embarrassed on top of it.

Mr. Trigg said very slowly and nicely, "Okay, whoever this is, just cry for a minute and don't try to talk. Then, when you're ready, I'll still be here waiting. I'm at my computer, so I can keep myself busy until you need me."

I cried a little more, with the phone tipped away from my mouth. Then I began to regain control. I took a few deep breaths. I swallowed, wishing Marcy was here with her mints and her Kleenex.

Finally, I said, "Mr. Trigg. It's Sam Martone."

"Ms. Martone! Whatever is the matter?" Mr. Trigg's voice was full of concern.

"Mr. Trigg, my . . . my advice backfired, and the person I gave it to is, um, kind of stalking me."

"Stalking you! Whatever do you *mean*?" I could hear the alarm in his voice.

"Well, first she sent me some mean letters at the Dear Know-It-All mailbox. Then she sent me a bunch of mean e-mails. Like, forty-two in a row last time I checked . . ."

"Forty-two e-mails! That's outrageous! I've been so busy since I got back, I haven't had a chance to check the Dear Know-It-All e-mails yet."

"Well, there may be more. I stopped checking a few days ago. But today she posted something on the high school's Buddybook wall that I should 'come out, come out, wherever I am.' I shuddered, just thinking of it again.

"My goodness!" Mr. Trigg shouted. "You're being cyberbullied! I'm calling Mr. Pfeiffer, and we'll get to the bottom of this! Oh, Ms. Martone, I wish you'd told me earlier!"

"But you were away! I didn't want to bother you!"

"Ms. Martone, this is a very serious matter. This is the very sort of thing you *should* bother me about! I hope you've told your mother!"

"Well . . . now I wish I had, but I thought I could handle it. Then when I knew I couldn't, I just kind of ignored it. But I guess that only made it grow bigger."

"Oh dear me, deary me! Alrighty, please, by all means, get your mother up to speed. I will speak with Mr. Pfeiffer, and then I will give her a ring on this number. . . . This is her mobile phone, correct?"

He pronounced it "MO-bye-ul." I had to smile a tiny bit. "Yes."

"Oh, and Ms. Martone, I am so very, very sorry that this happened to you. I am sorry that your term as Dear Know-It-All was so fraught and so brief. Now let's both run along. I don't want you to worry. You've done nothing wrong, and we're going to help fix this." And he hung up.

I sat in the hedge, staring at the MO-bye-ul in my hands. Then I realized he had said my term was "brief." He assumed I was quitting. That I was done with being Dear Know-It-All. Huh. I guessed I was. I waited to feel a huge relief, a weight lifted off my shoulders, but it didn't come. Maybe later it would, after I'd spoken to my mom and the grown-ups had sorted this out and dealt with it all. I was sure I'd feel better then.

Right?

Allie was in the kitchen in a flash when I opened the door. "How did it go?" she asked. Then she stopped dead in her tracks. "Wait! Did he make you cry? That little rat! I'm calling his brothers." She turned to stomp back up the stairs.

"No! Stop, Allie! I . . . chickened out. That's why I'm crying. I just . . . I chickened out." I shrugged and tried to look forlorn, so she'd feel pity instead of rage. It worked.

"Poor baby," she said, hugging me again. Wow,

between my tears and her hugs, we were breaking all sorts of records around here. "But maybe it's better. That outfit is all wrong."

My mom came in, freshly showered and changed into what she calls her "cozy clothes": leggings, a T-shirt, and socks. Her hair was up in a wet ponytail.

"Allie, I need to talk to mom now. In private, please," I said.

Allie looked at me and then at Mom, then back again. Finally she shrugged and said, "Whatever," and left.

I looked at Mom and said, "Can we go for a walk?"

"Love to," said my mom.

Once outside, and well away from Allie's window, I spilled my guts. I told my mom everything, and she just listened, asking a question here and there for clarity, but mostly just making appropriate noises. She was furious at Tired, and upset that I hadn't come to her sooner. When I finished she said, "Oh, honey," and she wrapped me in a big bear hug and rocked me from side to side. It felt good, but I didn't want anyone to see us.

"Later, Mom," I mumbled into her shoulder.

"Save this for home. I don't want anyone to see us and get suspicious."

"Right," she said, pulling away. "Look straight ahead and act natural," she added. I looked at her quickly to see if she was teasing me, but maybe she was getting into the spy thing just like Mr. Trigg.

"So you'll call Trigger when we get home?" I confirmed.

"Trigger?" My mom looked at me with a smile. "Oh, Mr. Trigg. Of course. And then I'm calling the principal. This is pretty serious, Samantha. I'm concerned."

"Oh, Mom, no, don't. It's not that bad."

My mom stopped dead in her tracks and turned to face me. "Yes it is that bad. It is, Sammy. What are you waiting for? For this person to track you down and . . . and, well, who knows what? This is a bully, Sam. A bully. She needs to be stopped. And she needs help. I'll be calling the principal, and maybe even the police, for both of your sakes."

"The police?" I shrieked. "But they can't come to the house. Allie will find out."

My mother was about to say, *Forget Allie*, I could tell. But then she reconsidered. "Fine. We won't blow your cover. But I'm going to school first thing tomorrow."

Oh boy.

"And I'm calling Mr. Trigg the second we get home."

When we got home, my mom sent Allie to get takeout for dinner and an ice-cream cake for dessert, which is my favorite. I guess Allie thought I looked so pathetic that she didn't even complain. "That ought to keep her out for a while," my mom said sternly. I smiled.

I sat in her office while she called Mr. Trigg, and she put us all on speaker phone. They exchanged details, and Mr. Trigg apologized profusely, then he filled us in on what was happening.

"Mr. Pfeiffer has been notified," said Mr. Trigg. "And we're having the school's IT person get into the server to see if he can identify who is sending the e-mails, using e-mail forensics."

"I have the letters that were dropped off here," Mom said. "I'll bring them in tomorrow."

"Excellent," said Mr. Trigg. "We can analyze the handwriting."

I knew that a small part of Trigger was loving the drama and the spy tactics. As bad as it all was, I had to smile again.

"Mrs. Martone, on behalf of the school and the paper, and just personally, I apologize from the bottom of my heart for what has happened to Sam. I would never have wanted something like this to happen and I am simply mortified I was away when it did."

I worried for a second that *he* was going to cry. "Keep calm and carry on, Mr. Trigg!" I said desperately, and he chuckled.

"You too, Ms. Martone. I'll get back to you as soon as we have any more information."

"Thanks, Paul," said my mother, and they both hung up.

"Lovely guy," she added, looking at the phone.

I nodded. "Yup."

"You never were totally sold on this column," my mom said, lost in thought.

"No," I agreed.

"It's going to be okay, Samantha," Mom said. "We're going to work this out. But you have to promise me that if anyone threatens or bullies you, you have to tell me as soon as possible. These things can escalate so quickly."

"I promise," I said.

The front door banged open.

"Dinner!" yelled Allie. "What a wild goose chase you sent me on!"

My mom and I looked at each other like the coconspirators we were. She winked at me, and we went up for dinner.

Chapter 11

JOURNALIST GRABS THE REINS, PULLS BACK FROM EDGE

★ ★ ★

I went to bed early, and my mom stayed up, talking to Mr. Pfeiffer and then Trigger again. The next morning, she went in to meet with them, to bring the letters and register a complaint, and thank goodness, I didn't have to go.

At my locker Hailey was breathless.

"Where have you been? I e-mailed and IM'd you all night last night!"

"Oh, I had a lot of work, and my mom got a special dinner. . . ."

"You of all people, offline! Anyway, I have major, major news!"

Oh boy. I was tired of major news. "Is this about Dear Know-It-All? 'Cause I heard all about that already." And the last thing I want to hear about is more school gossip.

Hailey looked at me like I was nuts.

Hailey continued. "What? No. I'm sick of that Know-It-All, anyway. No, this is way better. Are you ready?"

I sighed. Maybe I was losing my taste for news. Gossip, for sure. "What?" I said.

Hailey scowled at me. "You could try to be a little excited."

"Oh! This is good news? Okay, what then?" I made my voice peppier, and I smiled.

Hailey looked at me suspiciously. Then the news was too good to keep in so she gave up. "Guess who Scott Parker's cousin is?" Like Allie, she folded her arms across her chest and smiled a smug, closed-mouth smile at me.

"Justin Bieber?" I offered. I couldn't resist.

Hailey rolled her eyes. "No, no, no. Amanda Huxtable." She grinned.

"What?" It took a minute to sink in. "Hailey, that's such happy news! Woo-hoo! That's the best news I've heard all week!" I grabbed Hailey in a hug and danced her around, then I let go.

"Are you serious, Sam?" asked Hailey cautiously. "Are you really that happy for me?"

"Yes, Hailey. I am really that happy for you." I smiled to prove it.

"Wow. Thanks!"

"So what now?"

"I was going to ask you that question."

"Oh . . . I . . . I don't give advice anymore."

Hailey looked crestfallen. "*What*? But you give the *best* advice. Of anyone!"

Now it was my turn to roll my eyes. "Yeah, right." I turned to my locker to swap books.

"I'm serious!" said Hailey.

"Serious about what?" It was Michael. He'd come up behind us.

"Hey, Mikey!" I said, turning around. I was happy to see him. I think my greeting caught him off guard, but he looked really pleased and smiled a big smile back.

"So . . . I . . . Hey, want to go over everything this afternoon after school? Plot out the article?" he asked, seeming a little shy suddenly. Why, I have no idea.

"Totally," I said. "Why don't we meet . . . You know what? Why don't you just come over to my house. We'll meet outside and walk home together, okay?"

Now Michael was nodding and backing away, but he was still smiling. "Great. I'll meet you out front. See ya." Then he looked at Hailey. "What was so serious, by the way?"

"Don't you think Sam is good at giving advice?" Hailey said.

I could feel my face starting to get pink.

"Uh . . . I guess?" said Michael, looking confused.

"Well, she says she's not giving advice anymore, and I can't figure out why. And I need her to give me advice on something." Hailey narrowed her eyes at me. I looked away.

There was a pause, and I looked back to see Michael studying me curiously.

Then he shrugged. "Oh . . . well . . . Sounds like girl stuff. See you after school, Sam!" And he scooted down the hall, but not without giving me a worried look over his shoulder. Oh no. Did he know?

I turned to my locker and calmly began to take off my fleece and hang it up.

Hailey was standing there so quietly, I had to turn to look at her. She was smiling so hard, it looked like her face was going to crack.

"What?" I asked.

"You just asked him out! And he said yes!"

"*What?* I did *not*! That wasn't asking him out! He's just coming over to my house!"

"Well . . . you asked him *in*, then!" said Hailey, and we started laughing hysterically.

I laughed so hard, it almost turned to tears, but I stopped just in time. I'd had enough of that for one week. Or one month, even. *Journalist Grabs the Reins, Pulls Back from Edge.*

It felt good to be back in sync with Hailey. There was so much I couldn't tell her about what had been going on in my life, and it was frustrating. I felt guilty I didn't have much to offer her in return for her confessions about Scott Parker. Oh well, it would even out in the end. And soon I'd have Dear Know-It-All out of my life, and everything could go back to normal.

The day that had started off so well grew less well as it wore on. Everywhere I went I heard people chatting about the Tired of Waiting post. It was incredible how many people she had reached with this one snippet of text. I felt self-conscious everywhere I went because I had to guard my reaction to the information. When the girls in my math class (sorry, *numerics* class) were discussing it, I had to act like I couldn't remember what the column had been about, just to be safe. The only good thing was that people thought Tired was nuts.

"I mean, get over it!" said a girl named Stacey who I knew from Hailey's soccer team. I felt a little better after hearing that. Just a little.

"Do you think that we'll find out who Know-It-All is?" asked Isabella.

"Probably," said Stacey. "It sounds like Tired might already know who it is."

I shuddered. It was one thing to be the first Know-It-All to be found out. But what would Tired do if she knew it was me? Would she follow me home? Turn the whole school against me? My stomach started to hurt.

I was dying to stop by to see Mr. Trigg, but he and my mom and I had agreed on the phone that we wouldn't discuss anything about Tired of Waiting while we were at school. However, by the end of the day, I was so nervous, I couldn't take it anymore. So I stopped by on my way out to meet Michael.

"Hey, Mr. Trigg!" I called.

"Ms. Martone! How lovely to see you!"

I went over to his office and stood in the doorway. "How was your trip?" It was like we really were spies, saying lines that didn't matter but that covered up the real business at hand.

"Lovely, just lovely," he said. "I saw Mr. Lawrence. He told me you two have had some very interesting developments in the lunch story."

I nodded. "We're meeting after school today to map it all out and then we'll pop by tomorrow to run it by you."

"Excellent." He smiled. "Remember not to just condemn the food. Find out what goes into it, the process—all of it."

"Oh, we will all right. It's really shaping up." I stood there, not wanting to leave yet.

There was so much for us to say to each other. I rocked from foot to foot and twisted my hair with one hand, which I sometimes do when I get really anxious. Mr. Trigg cleared his throat. There was no one else around. "Ms. Martone, thanks for trying," he said quietly. "I'm working on your replacement now. Hate to see you quit, but wouldn't have it any other way."

I stood, rooted to the spot.

Know-It-All would be over for me. I wouldn't have to hide things anymore. I wouldn't have to worry about anyone getting mad. But quit. Quit? *Quit!* I had never quit anything before. Even when I went to tennis camp with Hailey and was so bad that all I did was chase balls for most of the two weeks, I hung in there. I did want to end the bullying by Tired. But I didn't want to quit something because of her. Besides, I didn't remember actually quitting. It was *my* column. Mr. Trigg gave it to *me.*

You know what? I wasn't going to let this bully win! Before I knew it, I was blurting, "Mr. Trigg, I didn't quit. I don't quit. I'll have a new column for you in three days."

I spun on my heel before he could say anything to stop me, then I rushed out the door without looking back. Outside of the school, Michael was waiting for me (thank goodness, because it meant I didn't have to walk home alone). I was so confused about what just happened with Mr. Trigg, and really nervous that I accidentally asked Michael out, that I just started babbling. Michael listened with an amused smile on his face as we walked. I only wished I could tell him everything. Maybe someday I would, but not now.

At home I opened the door and called "Hel-looo!" I figured Allie was there. She always got home before me. But today she wasn't.

"Samantha?" Mom called from downstairs.

"Yes!" I called. "It's me. And Michael," I added in case she was going to talk about Know-It-All. She came up the stairs and looked surprised, then she smiled.

"Hi, Michael!" she said. "It's nice to meet you."

"It's nice to meet you, too, Mrs. Martone." Michael shook her hand, and she beamed. Mom was a sucker for good manners.

"Sam, I have to run an errand, and I didn't want you to be home alone. You guys okay here, just the two of you?" I could feel myself blushing. She didn't have to make such a big deal about us being alone.

"We're fine, Mom!" I said, and I opened the door to shoo her out. We waved good-bye and I shut the door and then it was just the two of us. It was just a little awkward being alone in my house with Michael. He seemed awkward too.

"Let's . . . get a snack, okay?" I said, and we trooped up the stairs to the kitchen.

"Cool multilevel house," he said.

"Thanks. What do you like? Cheese and crackers? A salami sandwich? Cookies?" What did boys like to eat? I knew Michael liked to bake cinnamon buns, but I didn't have anything like that. I looked around the counter. "Oh! A Mrs. Moseby bar!"

As soon as I spied those, it broke the ice, and we began chatting away, talking about Mary Bonner, munching on her bars, plotting out the article—smooth sailing.

Just as we were at our most relaxed, in came Allie with a bang.

"Well, well, well, who have we here?" she said, entering the kitchen. I glared at her. She knew perfectly well who we had here.

Michael stood up to greet her (great manners as usual) and she all but patted him on the head. "You *are* adorable, just like everyone says!" She had a sly smile on her face, but thank goodness did not look at me to indicate that I was "everyone."

Michael was bashful, and deflected the compliment. He smiled slightly and looked away.

"I know your brothers pretty well," Allie offered, batting her eyes. "Nice guys."

"Thanks," said Michael.

And then, thank heavens, her phone rang and we were dead to her. But as she left the room, she called over her shoulder, "You still haven't told me who Dear Know-It-All is!"

Aaack! I have never wanted to be an only child so badly in my life.

I laughed it off, but Michael looked serious.

"Did you hear about that post yesterday?" he asked.

"How could I not? It's all anyone could talk about today. Bo-ring!" I was trying to play it off really casually and move on, but I noticed my hands started to shake. I sat on them.

Michael looked at me. "That was some serious stuff. Scary, I think. I hope they catch the kid who did it." He shook his head.

I nodded, looking down, like I was having a sad moment for the people involved, but I didn't say anything. I was worried if I opened my mouth, I'd blurt it all out. Or start to cry.

Then, out of nowhere, Michael said, "Hey, the other day, when you were saying you were wrong about someone . . . Did you . . . did you mean me? Are you, like, not into us working together any-more?"

I looked up in surprise. Michael was biting his lip and actually looked worried. He stared down at his fingernails.

"No! *What?* Are you kidding? I totally love you!"

Michael's head snapped up like he'd been electrocuted. His eyes were wide with shock.

Oh my gosh, oh my gosh. Did I just tell Michael Lawrence that I loved him???

Fix this! Fix this! I thought in desperation.

Strangely enough, a smile began to bloom on his face. Maybe it was a nervous I-can't-believe-what-a-nerd-you-are smile.

Girl Prays for Lightning to Strike Her.

I stammered, "I mean . . . I mean . . . I love *working* with you! You're the best partner a girl could have!" I smacked my forehead and kind of fake laughed, shaking my head from side to side. "Writing partner!" I added. Ugh.

Michael laughed too, in a kind of forced way. "Oh, right. Yeah. No. I know what you mean. I love working with you, too. Totally. Yeah. So . . ."

"Anyway," I said, chuckling. What I was really thinking was that there is not a bigger loser in all the world than me. Not one. Or, okay, one. Tired of Waiting was a bigger loser.

"Yeah. Anyway . . ." said Michael.

Awkward! Awkward! What to say? The gears

in my head spun, not making any headway.

"Hi girls!" my mother trilled, walking in the front door downstairs.

"And boy!" I called, so thrilled for the distraction. Yep, there was a boy in my house. And he was there for me. Maybe this day wasn't a total disaster after all.

Chapter 12

FATIGUE SETS IN AS BATTLE WINDS DOWN

★ ★ ★

All in all, the afternoon with Michael went well. We mapped out the whole article, made a list (or I did; he just keeps it in his head) of loose ends we needed to tie up: a quote from Mr. Pfeiffer the principal, a tiny bit more research on state lunch regulations, and a few other minor details. It felt good to be hanging out together. It was like we had progressed to a new stage in our friendship or whatever it was.

Allie was going to a homecoming pep rally that night, so my mom and I were free to talk. She filled me in on her visit to school. It had been brief. Mr. Pfeiffer and the IT guy had identified the computer where the e-mails were coming from, and Mr. Pfeiffer and Mr. Trigg were contacting the parents of the girl to whom that computer was registered. Once they confirmed who Tired was, she'd probably be suspended because there was a zero-tolerance policy on bullying.

Part of me felt really sorry for Tired, and I talked to my mom about it.

"Imagine how lonely she is, using a newspaper column for advice, and then getting so vicious and relentless about it. I still feel guilty for starting the whole thing," I said.

My mother shook her head. "First of all, you didn't start it," she said firmly. "She wrote asking for advice, and she was the one who escalated it. You know, honey, this girl clearly has a lot of issues, and this whole incident, or series of incidents, was really just a cry for help. It wasn't your advice that made her go a little cuckoo. She was already there. This was just a trigger."

I smiled at the word "trigger." "I love Mr. Trigg, by the way," I said.

My mother nodded. "Yes, but I'm pretty mad at him right now, and I told him as much earlier.

He made a bad judgment call giving you direct access to the mail and e-mail. He should always be filtering that stuff, no matter where he is. If he's away, it can just wait. It's too much responsibility, too much liability, for someone your age."

I hated to point a finger at Mr. Trigg, but she did have a point. "I guess you're right," I said. I sighed. I was tired of all this. Tired of Tired. **_Fatigue Sets in as Battle Winds Down._**

"I'm going to bed," I said.

"Love you, honey," said my mom. "Sleep well." She planted a kiss on my head, and I went up.

I had an IM from Hailey.

SP said hi to me today in the hall.

I wrote back.

You go, girl!

But whatever you do, don't ask him out, I added silently.

Then I turned off my computer and went to

bed. It was only eight thirty, but I fell asleep right away and slept all night.

I didn't see Hailey until lunch the next day. She was ecstatic. She gestured to her tray, where three plates of partially eaten cookies sat.

"Oh my gosh! Have you tried these?" she mumbled through a mouth full of crumbs.

I looked closely. Compost cookies!

"Why, yes I have," I said. "I didn't see them up there."

Hailey shook her head and finished chewing. She swallowed hard, forcing it. "They're not part of the official school lunch. They're a 'bonus' item, like a supplement, you can buy at that little table over there." She pointed toward the door to the kitchen where the little table from Mary Bonner's office was set up with its striped tablecloth. My eyes nearly popped out of my head! I jumped up and ran over. Carmen was manning the table.

"Hey, Carmen!" I said. "What's up?"

"Hi, Sam! Well, Mary spoke with Mr. Pfeiffer

about some new plans for the cafeteria, and one of the things they decided was that we'd offer a bonus item for sale at lunch every day. The revenue will pay for the ingredients for upcoming bonus items."

"Wow! Cool! How much for two cookies?" I asked.

"A dollar," said Carmen.

Pretty good price. I bought the cookies. "This must make a lot more work for you guys," I said.

Carmen shook her head and beamed. "It doesn't matter. Just seeing the kids' faces when they're eating something they love, it's worth it. Of course we're launching with cookies, but over the next few weeks we're going to work our way into mixing it up with superhealthy snacks and side dishes, like kale chips and hard-boiled eggs. Maybe even some main courses, like veggie wraps and stuff. We figured we'd lure you all in early with treats and get you in the habit of stopping by this table!" She winked at me.

"That's great," I said. "Well, good luck! And thanks. Bye!"

As I walked away, Jeff was approaching the

table. I saw him squint at Carmen's name tag and say, "Hey, Carmen! I'm Jeff. I'd like to buy some cookies, please."

I had to smile. Now Bob, Carmen, Marcy, and Mary would be known by everyone. And all it took was trying out a new idea. Of course, it helped that they launched with the compost cookies!

Back at my lunch table, Hailey had finished her cookie-based lunch.

I looked sideways at her. "You know, you said yourself that the idea is that these bonus items 'supplement' the existing lunch."

"Well, my existing lunch would have been the cookies," she reasoned. "So I'm just *supplementing* them with a few more. Anyway, guess what? I joined the chess club. I've always wanted to learn how to play. I think it will help with my soccer strategy, don't you?" She was talking a mile a minute, wired on sugar.

I narrowed my eyes suspiciously. "Wait, let me guess. Scott Parker is in the chess club, right?"

Hailey was the picture of innocence. "What? I don't know. Maybe. Well, yes. Okay, but that's not the reason I joined. Not the only reason, anyway."

"Right," I said, laughing. "So why did you join?"

"Shut up. It's going to be interesting."

"I'm sure it will be fascinating," I said, still smiling as I ate some buttered rice.

"Well, how's *your* love life progressing? How was your date yesterday?"

"I wouldn't exactly call it a 'date,'" I said, lowering my voice. "I did the dumbest thing." I told Hailey about how I'd accidentally declared my love to Michael.

Hailey covered her mouth with both hands, she was laughing so hard. "Oh, Sammy! You didn't!"

I shook my head. "Yes, I did. Can you believe it?"

"That's even more extreme than asking a guy out on a date!" she said, laughing.

"Ugh. Don't remind me," I said. Oops.

"Remind you about what?" Hailey asked.

Oh, I really wanted to tell her everything! I hated the secrets between us now. "Oh, just—"

And then who should walk by but Scott Parker, bless his little heart. "Hey, Hailey," he said as he walked by. The way he said it was kind of flat, like he was greeting her out of duty or something, but for a shy guy like him, I knew it was a major step for him to speak first, and especially when Hailey was sitting with a friend.

Hailey, however, was speechless. I kicked her gently under the table, and she got my drift. "Oh, hey, Scott! How's it going?"

"Good." He nodded, and he kept walking.

We didn't move a muscle to watch him walk away, though I know we both wanted to—especially Hailey! Instead we raised our eyebrows really high and looked sideways at each other with big smiles on our faces. *Thaw Begins in Frozen Crush.*

"Yay, Hails!" I said.

"Do you think that means he likes me?" she whispered.

"Seems like it!" I said cautiously.

"So what do I do now?" Hailey was beside herself.

I flashed back to my mother's advice from a week ago (had it really only been a week? It felt like months). Keep your advice open-ended. Don't tell people to do anything you wouldn't do.

"Just take it nice and slow," I advised. "Let

it develop naturally." *Whatever you do, don't ask him out*, I added silently.

That night I sat down at my computer to write the Dear Know-It-All column without an idea of what I would say. It took a while (okay, I was procrastinating, checking all the news sites, reading blogs, including Mrs. Moseby), but when it came, it came in a big fat rush. I read it and reread it until my eyes were blurry. It was a little raw and unpolished, but I kind of liked it like that. I took one last read and then I pushed send, and off it went to Mr. Trigg for editing.

Here is what it said:

Dear Tired of Waiting,

I am sorry things worked out for you the way they did, and I am sorry my advice to you was bad. Looking back, it seems like you ignored the fact that your crush didn't like you right from the beginning. Then you took my advice, and it made things worse, and for that I apologize. But to turn around and bully me for it, both in private and in public, as well as anonymously, was cowardly, dangerous, and hurtful.

I am doing the best that I can with this column. I give the best possible advice I can give, based on my very limited knowledge of a situation. I try hard, and I try to give active solutions. I try to be positive, and I try to be right. Sometimes I'm wrong, and I admit it. But I don't hide behind taunting or bullying or public shaming. I know that there is a real live person writing to me, just as I expect people to understand the same about me on this end. Just because we're all anonymous in this column doesn't mean none of us has feelings.

The worst thing in life is to not take chances or try new things. It leaves you stagnant, and you can't grow or change the world in your own special way. Most people try, and some try hard, to change things they don't like. Complaining might feel good, but it's not productive. It's better to try to be part of a solution than sit around criticizing something. Someone with more guts than you might have said, "Hey, I tried something, and it didn't work. Let's share this information so others can learn from it." But no, instead you holed up and just tormented me from a distance. I can't help someone like you.

To everyone else out there, keep on trying to change the world for the better. Stay strong, and don't let the bullies get you down. And no matter what, never suffer in silence.

Yours truly,

Dear Know-It-All

Chapter 13

JOURNALISTS EFFECT CHANGE FOR THE BETTER

★ ★ ★

When the next issue of the *Cherry Valley Voice* came out, the school was electric with feedback. Everyone was talking about the Dear Know-It-All rebuttal, cheering when they read it, and high-fiving. I felt great witnessing it. And Mr. Pfeiffer told Mr. Trigg that three different kids had come to him to report bullying, and while he wasn't glad to hear it, he was glad they'd come. Even more, they'd come with friends who were there for moral support. That detail made me feel even better. No one should suffer alone.

The lunch article was a smash hit too, and since Mr. Trigg had agreed it should be part of an ongoing series, we would continue to check back in. He also noted that it would help keep things moving and developing if the administration knew they were going to be held accountable for their progress in the paper every other week.

What ended up happening, besides the creation of the bonus item every day, was Mr. Pfeiffer and the science department agreed to incorporate a greenhouse growing unit into next term's Earthonomics class. We'll be growing six kinds of herbs, and Mary will come in once a week to demonstrate recipes using the herbs. Then we'll get to vote on what we like, and she'll incorporate the recipe into the "bonus" item rotation. *Journalists Effect Change for the Better.*

Michael Lawrence saw me in the hall and gave me a high five. "You did it again!" He smiled.

"Well, *we* did it again!" I said.

"Yeah," he said. "We did. But you really did the right thing."

I froze. Did Michael know?

"Just out of Earthonomics class," said Michael. "It's going to be way more fun in the next couple weeks!"

Whew. I think.

At the library I e-mailed Allie an electronic copy of the lunch article, with photos, so she could post it as a PDF download on the high-school website. With Mrs. Moseby's website so popular over there, it made sense that the older kids should know about the other half of Mary Bonner's life.

Meanwhile, Mr. Pfeiffer and Mary are going to take this year (I know, it seems like a long time, but at least they're trying!) to develop a new lunch plan that will pass government muster. I am pretty hopeful they'll get it through, even if they have to do it in some kooky backdoor way—like the way Mr. Pfeiffer got the new curriculum approved. You've got to give that guy credit. He does try.

And speaking of trying, the day after the latest issue of the *Cherry Valley Voice* came out, Hailey grabbed me in the hall and dragged me into the ladies' room. She checked under every stall and under the sinks (which I thought was a little extreme) to make sure no one was in there. I flashed back to my Dear Know-It-All spy games and I gave a little shudder. Finally, feeling secure, Hailey began to whisper.

"So I went to chess club yesterday, and guess who I got paired up against?"

"Oh, Hailey, that's great! How did it go? Was he—"

"Shh! Stop talking!" said Hailey.

I clammed up.

"He told me an unbelievable story. So get this. There was this really aggressive girl in his Spanish class. I didn't know who she was, and now I can't remember her name. Miranda something. I think I blocked it out. Anyway, she was always following him around, and then she started leaving notes in his locker, and then little creepy pink teddy bears and candy and stuff. He didn't like her to start with, but after a while, he started to kind of hate her. It was a little scary. . . ."

Oh my gosh. I think I knew where this was going, but I couldn't say anything yet.

"So after a while, it's like she became sort of a bully. Like a love bully. All his friends would kind of laugh at her, but Scott was scared because when he finally told her he didn't like her at all, she just got more relentless. Then one day she asked him out on a date, and it really freaked him. He told all his friends, and they laughed it off, but she was angry, and then she felt like everyone knew. So she started to kind of stalk him and be mean to him, like on Buddybook and stuff like that. And that's why his cousin Amanda would meet him to walk him home every day. Because he was scared, but he didn't want to tell his friends."

I thought I was going to faint. I sank down against the wall and put my head on my knees. Oh my gosh.

"Hey, Sam. Are you okay? Hey!" Hailey squatted next to me and patted my arm. "What's the matter?"

"Oh, it's just . . ."

I had to tell her! She was my best friend! She could keep a secret. No one would ever find out. I just couldn't do this alone anymore!

But the door to the bathroom banged open, and a group of sixth graders came in to check themselves in the mirror, and the moment passed.

"I know it's a scary story, but, come on, get up

off the floor at least," said Hailey.

I stood weakly, and she brought me a wet paper towel and began patting my face and the back of my neck with it.

The sixth graders were oblivious, so Hailey kept talking in a quiet voice. "Anyway, when the Dear Know-It-All came out the other day, Scott read it and it changed his life, he said. It gave him courage, and he decided he'd better at least *try* to do something about this bully. So he went to Mr. Pfeiffer's office with Amanda and his best friend, Joe Proctor, and they told him the whole story. And now the girl is being suspended indefinitely, but she has to come to school to talk with a counselor once a week."

Oh no. *Suspended indefinitely?* I started to feel worse, but then I remembered that my mom did say Tired—or Miranda, rather—clearly needed help. I guess it was for the best. I really hoped she would get help. Boys could really make you crazy.

"Wow. Poor Scott," I said,

Hailey nodded, serious. "I know. I feel so bad for him."

"So I guess that's why he's so cautious with girls," I said.

Hailey nodded again. "Uh-huh. He's really sweet. Do you think it means he likes me, if he told me that story?"

I thought for a minute. This poor guy had enough on his plate without some new girl crushing on him hard. "Hailey, it means you're his *friend*," I said firmly. "And that's pretty darn great. For now, I think that's the best you'll get. Don't push the poor guy."

Hailey stared off into space, lost in thought. "Yeah . . . I just hope I don't get tired of waiting. . . . I may just have to ask him out," she said.

I turned to her in a panic. "Hailey!" I cried. The sixth graders all went silent and turned to look at us.

But Hailey was laughing. "Kidding! I'm just kidding!" she trilled. "Let's go."

I ran into Michael at the bonus table at lunch. We were both buying baked kale chips from Bob. (I know, kale sounds gross, right? But it's actually really good as chips!)

"Hey, Pasty!" said Michael. "Stocking up on some snacks to keep that tummy quiet?"

"Oh, shush, you!" I said, but he *did* make me laugh.

"Saw Trigger this morning. He's pretty psyched about the lunch article."

"Oh, I have to stop by to see him. When's our next staff meeting again?"

"Tomorrow after school."

"Right. Well, I'll pop in today, then. I can't wait that long to hear what he thinks."

"Hey, what are you up to later? Like after school today? We have a short practice because they don't want to tire us out before the homecoming game this weekend. I was thinking . . . Do you to come over and brainstorm some ideas for stories? I can make my world-famous cinnamon buns while we're thinking. I know you work better when your stomach is full."

Was this a date? Was Michael Lawrence asking me out? Or was he asking me *in*? Uh-oh. I started to laugh.

But then his face fell. "Or whatever, sorry. I'm

sure you're really busy and stuff, so maybe . . ."

I swatted him. "Of course I'd love to come. It just made me laugh because of an inside joke I have with Hailey. Anyway, count me in! I'll go to the library and knock off some homework while you practice."

Michael still looked nervous. "I hope the joke's not about me?" he said.

"Oh, no." Lie, lie, lie. "It's about . . . buns!" I blurted. Oh no! Even worse! And I felt my face turning red. "But not your buns! I mean. Oh gosh. Just . . . I'll see you after school." I turned on my heel like an idiot and raced off.

"Bye, Sam!" Bob called after me. How mortifying. He'd witnessed the whole thing! But at least he wasn't anonymous anymore.

I turned around and waved with a dorky smile. "Bye, Bob! Thanks for the chips!"

"Anytime!" he replied.

I had fifteen minutes before my next class, so I took the opportunity to pop into Trigger's office.

He was there.

"Hey, Mr. Trigg!" I called, crossing the newsroom.

"Ms. Martone! I'm so happy to see you! Do come in!" he replied.

I went and stood in his doorway as I had countless times before.

He pushed back his chair and clasped his hands across his middle. "Ms. Martone, what a wonderful issue of the *Cherry Valley Voice* we have this week. And much thanks are due to you."

I could feel myself blushing. "It was . . . an interesting process," I said.

"Not an ideal one," said Mr. Trigg sadly.

"Is the girl . . . is she going to be all right?" I asked in a whisper.

Mr. Trigg nodded firmly. "Yes, in fact, she was relieved to have been brought in and given some help. Now she's on a better track."

"I just feel so guilty all the time," I said, wincing as I thought of the pain I'd accidentally caused Scott Parker.

"Ms. Martone, none of this was your fault. It had been going on for quite some time before you got involved. And your reaction to all of it has done a world of good for this community. Look, weeding out the bad guys and calling them on their crimes . . . That's what the very *best* journalists do!"

"I guess," I said. "It's not exactly objective journalism."

"Pshaw!" said Mr. Trigg dismissively. "It's journalistic activism, and you're quite adept at it. I'd say you're one of the lucky few who has found her calling at quite a young age." He smiled at me. "Now, in the words of the immortal Winston Churchill, 'Let us go forward together.'"

I grinned. "Thanks, Mr. Trigg. Will do!"

As I left his office, that same old poster caught my eye and gave me the usual thrill.

"*Your* Courage, *Your* Cheerfulness, *Your* Resolution Will Bring Us Victory."

You're darn right, I thought. I strode out the door to Earthonomics with a spring in my step. Life was good.

That afternoon, I left the library with butterflies in my stomach. I was going to Michael Lawrence's house! I ducked into the girls' room, combed my hair, and checked my teeth in the mirror (to make sure there wasn't any food stuck in them). I pinched my cheeks to brighten them, and I smiled at myself. I felt happier than I had in more than a week.

Back in the hall I turned a corner to reach my locker, and ahead I spied a familiar figure, lounging by the water fountain. My heart skipped a beat.

"What's up, Paste?" called Michael. He looked supercute in his work-out clothes from football practice. His hair was tousled and his cheeks were pink, and I could see his arm muscles under his T-shirt sleeves.

"Hey, Mikey," I said, very cool, but inside I was bursting with joy that this hottie was waiting for me.

"Ready for our plan?"

"Yup. Looking forward to it!" *Do not talk about buns, do not talk about buns*, I warned myself.

"Great, 'cause I'm tired of waiting!"

Wait, *what*? I looked up at him quickly, and he was smiling at me.

"Are you?" I asked, my stomach clenching as everything came back to me.

"Nah, I could never get tired of waiting for you," he said with a wink.

Then I fainted, and he had to revive me.

Just kidding.

I giggled and hoisted my messenger bag onto my shoulder and wondered for about the hundredth time if he knew I was Dear Know-It-All. Well, if he does know . . . maybe that would be okay. As long as he doesn't blow my cover, and as long as he keeps looking this good and feeding me, I think we'll be all right.

"Let's hit it," he said.

"Righty-ho!" I said, imitating Trigger. And we both laughed.

All's Well That Ends Well for Rookie Journo.

Cherry

THE CHERRY VALLEY MIDDLE SCHOOL NEWS

★ WANT THE SCOOP ★

ON WHAT SAMANTHA IS UP TO NEXT?

★ ★ ★

Here's a sneak peek of the third book in the

DEAR KNOW-IT-ALL!

series:

A Level Playing Field

MARTONE A BORN WALLFLOWER!

Hailey came over after soccer practice so I could help her with her homework. We followed our usual routine: I offered Hailey a snack. She declined. I made myself a snack. Hailey ate it. Then we got down to business. Talking about boys, that is.

"I get to write another article with super-hunk!" I cried.

Hailey was munching on a cracker with melted cheddar cheese. "What else is new?" she said, spraying crumbs all over her plate. "Oops!" She laughed, spraying some more.

I rolled my eyes. "Why 'what else is new'?" I asked.

"You guys are totally a team at this point. It's like . . . a given that you write everything together. You're like . . . peanut butter and jelly. Like . . . cheddar cheese and crackers!" Hailey laughed again and crammed the last cracker in her mouth.

"You think?" I couldn't suppress my smile.

Hailey nodded, her mouth too full to speak.

"Really?" I could talk about this forever. I wondered if other people thought we went together like that.

Finally Hailey swallowed. "Really," she said, nodding her head hard.

I grinned again. "Wow."

"Are you going to ask him to dance?" said Hailey.

What?

"What do you mean?" I asked.

"At the school dance next Friday! Duh!"

"Wait, that's *next Friday*?!" I started to panic. "How can it be? Already?" I jumped up and ran to the calendar by the kitchen desk. There it was. *November 18. School Dance/Sam*, it said in green ink.

My stomach got all clenchy, and I had to sit down.

"Aren't you psyched?" asked Hailey. "I am!"

"No. Definitely not psyched. More like terrified! What if no one asks me to dance?"

I put my head down on my arms and shook it from side to side. I imagined another headline: *Martone a Born Wallflower.* "You'll be busy dancing with Scott Parker, and I'll be all by myself."

"Scott who?" asked Hailey, perplexed.

I looked up. "Scott *Parker*? Hello? Crush of your life? Obsession of the year?"

Hailey laughed. "Oh, *Scott*! Scott *Parker*!" She waved her hand dismissively. "I'm totally over him. He's too shy. Anyway, he had that weird stalker, and I'm just going to stay away from him and that whole scenario with a ten-foot pole!"

I had to laugh. "Okay, so who *are* you going to dance with?"

"You!" Hailey jumped up and turned on the iPod on the counter. Hailey began doing a really funny dance, all rubbery arms with her head pumping up and down. I couldn't help laughing.

Hailey stopped. "Why are you laughing? Do I look funny dancing?"

"Wait, um . . . I thought you were just fooling around."

"No, that's my real dance," she said. "Is it bad? Do I look like a total geek?"

"Oh! Oh no. Totally not. No. It's fine. It's . . . well, Hailey, actually . . . we have some work to do." I went over to the iPod. When I found a song I liked, I turned it way up loud and began to dance.

"C'mon, just copy me," I instructed.

Hailey watched me out of the corner of her eye and began trying to imitate my moves. We shook our hips from side to side and gave a little wiggle to the right, a wiggle to the left, and I pumped my bent arms at my side.

Hailey and I looked at each other, and I knew we were thinking the same thing. *We need dance lessons! And fast!*